Zoey felt as though she'd just been given an electroshock treatment. This gorgeous, intelligent, talented, perfect guy had never had a girlfriend. "Why?"

Aaron picked up the guitar again and began tuning.

"Well, I don't really believe in sex before marriage. And these days that's not exactly considered a desirable quality in a boyfriend."

If Zoey felt shocked before, she now felt as if she'd been run over by a steamroller. She didn't try to stop herself from placing her hand gently on Aaron's shoulder. "I can relate, Aaron."

He squeezed her hand. "Can you really?"

She nodded. "Yeah. It's something Lucas and I fight about all the time. He just doesn't understand that I'm not ready."

Aaron gazed into her eyes. "I wish . . . I wish I'd met you somewhere else, Zoey. You're the kind of girl I've been waiting all my life to meet."

Titles in the MAKING OUT series

1. Zoey fools around
2. Jake finds out
3. Nina won't tell
4. Ben's in love
5. Claire gets caught
6. What Zoey saw
7. Lucas gets hurt
8. Aisha goes wild
9. Zoey plays games
10. Nina shapes up   March 1996
11. Ben takes a chance   April 1996
12. Claire can't lose   May 1996
13. Don't tell Zoey   June 1996
14. Aaron lets go   July 1996

*And more fabulous MAKING OUT
books will follow!*

Zoey plays games

KATHERINE APPLEGATE

Pan Books

Cover photography by Jutte Klee

First published 1996 by Macmillan Children's Books
a division of Macmillan Publishers Limited
25 Eccleston Place, London SW1W 9NF
and Basingstoke

Associated companies throughout the world

ISBN 0 330 34779 9

135798642

A CIP catalogue record for this book is available from
the British Library.

Printed and bound in Great Britain by
Mackay's of Chatham, Kent

Zoey

What do I have to be
thankful for? If you'd
asked me that question a
few weeks ago, I would
have said nothing,
nothing, and nothing. A
person doesn't tend to be
grateful when she finds
out her mother is having
an affair. She's even less
grateful when it turns out
her father has a so-called
love child wandering
around Maine. And then
there's the matter of Lucas
making out with his ex,
Claire. None of these facts
would make a girl want to
dress up like a Pilgrim
and eat stuffed turkey with

her friends and family.

Luckily, today isn't a few weeks ago. My parents have rediscovered their burning passion for each other. On a down note, they're displaying that passion in such a manner as to make me positively embarrassed. My brother, Benjamin, is lucky he can't see it. I mean, I love to read about pounding hearts, zinging blood, and loud, wet kisses in romance novels — but witnessing those things between your own parents isn't natural. Is it?

And Lucas and I are more in love than ever. If I was totally honest, I might even admit that we

disgust a few people with
our public displays of
affection. But that's
natural for teenagers.
Isn't it?

LUCAS

Am I thankful? You could say that. I'm thankful that Claire owned up to the fact that it was her, not me, who was driving the car the night Wade McRoyan was killed. (The fact that she let me go through two years of reform school before coming clean doesn't taint my gratitude. Not at all.)

What else am I thankful for? Three things. Zoey, Zoey, and Zoey. Oh, yeah — did I mention Zoey?

Nina

America, America, God shed his grace on thee . . . Or is it me? I never did get that song.

Ah, Thanksgiving. Such a wonderful holiday. The one day of the year when we get to stuff our faces and celebrate the exploitation of an entire race of people. See, a few hundred years ago, a whole bunch of Pilgrims came over to the New World to get away from religious persecution. (Later, we got all the people who were about to go to jail but got put on a rickety old boat instead.)

The Pilgrims had a pretty tough

time of it. There wasn't a lot of food, the weather sucked, and TV had not yet been invented. So one day the Indians (I'm talking good, nice Indians, not the screaming, tomahawk-wielding ones we see in movies) invited the Pilgrims to share a feast. Well, the Pilgrims were thankful for the grub, and for the fact that none of the Indians (known to the politically correct as Native Americans) had tried to scalp them. Since then, we've had this tradition called Thanksgiving. I'd say how bogus it is, except that someone might listen to me and cancel the whole deal. Then we wouldn't get the day off from school anymore.

Anyway, I'm thankful for a few things. For example, as a junior in high school, I've passed that age when your class does an ultradumb Thanksgiving play. In third grade I was the turkey. Mrs. Atkinson tried to convince me that being the turkey was an honor. Ha! I had to wear orange tights and an extremely uncomfortable papier-mâché turkey body. Of course, when Claire did the same play the year before, she was the beautiful Indian princess. That same year Zoey was

the saintly Pilgrim mother. No big
surprise that after all this time,
I still feel like a turkey.

And I'm thankful that I
started going out with Benjamin.

Let me say that again. I, Nina
Geiger, am going out with Benjamin
Passmore. He's, like, my boyfriend
with a capital B. And as far as
that's concerned, I'm thankful
with a capital T.

Claire

Thankful? That's an interesting concept. I'll have to think about it sometime.

One

Zoey Passmore stretched lazily as she sat up in bed. Since she'd woken two hours earlier, she'd been lying in bed, nestled under her thick comforter. If it had been a regular Thursday, she'd have been in algebra already.

But it was Thanksgiving, one of those treasured holidays when kids across America lounged in bed, happy to be alive for the simple reason that they were missing school.

The hardwood floor of her room felt like ice as Zoey crossed the room from her bed to her dresser. She pulled a pair of wool L.L. Bean socks out of the top drawer, anticipating their warmth. Balancing on first one foot and then the other, Zoey pulled on the socks.

"Great outfit," she said aloud, glancing down at herself. The red socks clashed with the semi-short maroon Boston Bruins nightshirt she always wore to bed.

She moved to stand in front of her full-length mirror. As she'd expected, she looked like a young, half-crazy bag lady. Her dark blond hair was a tangled mess, and there was yellow gunk in the corners of her blue eyes. To make matters worse, she had the beginnings of a lone zit on her left cheek.

"The stubble on your legs is a nice touch," a husky voice said behind her.

Zoey spun around and saw Lucas Cabral's head. He was still standing in the hall, but he'd opened the door and stuck his head inside her bedroom.

"Lucas! I could have been naked in here," Zoey said. She pulled the door open the rest of the way and put a hand on her hip.

He wiggled his eyebrows suggestively. "That was sort of the idea, Zo."

Zoey sighed with frustration. The expression "one-track mind" was an understatement in Lucas's case. He probably thought about sex more often than he breathed.

Still, he looked awfully cute at the moment. Zoey's eyes traveled from his tousled blond hair to his dark eyes. Even this early in the morning, Lucas's eyes were smoldering with desire. When her gaze dropped to his full red lips, Zoey took a step back to let him come in. There weren't many occasions when Zoey could resist those lips.

Lucas walked into the bedroom and gently kicked the door shut with his foot. Zoey felt a familiar flutter in her stomach as Lucas looked into her eyes. He put his hands on her hips, running his fingers over the thin material of her nightshirt.

"I haven't brushed my teeth yet," Zoey

whispered as he brought his face close to hers.

Lucas didn't answer. He brushed her lips lightly with his, then pulled her close. Zoey's arms found their way to his neck, his hair, his face. As the kiss became more intense, Zoey forgot all about morning breath.

After ten minutes of kissing in a tangled heap on her bed, Zoey pulled away. She knew where making out with Lucas led, and it was too early in the morning for *that* argument.

"Where are you going?" Lucas asked. His voice was tight and high-pitched, as if he were being strangled.

Zoey stood next to the bed and tugged on the bottom of her Bruins nightshirt. "I have to get dressed, Lucas."

He groaned and rolled over onto his stomach. "I like you just the way you are." He stuck out an arm and tried to reach for her hand. "Why don't you come back here?"

Zoey let him pull her back over to the bed, but she didn't lie down. She perched stiffly at the edge of the mattress. "Lucas, it's Thanksgiving. Can we call a sex truce at least for today?"

He held up his hands. "Peace, babe. I'll be on my best behavior for the next twenty-four hours."

"Thank you." Zoey leaned over and kissed Lucas softly on the cheek. "Now, will you go bug Benjamin for a while? I have to be showered, dressed, and at the restaurant in, like, an hour."

Zoey grinned as she listened to Lucas's footsteps retreating down the stairs. So far, the events of the morning had been infinitely better than algebra class.

Nina Geiger glared into her closet, yanking hanger after hanger to the side. Red plaid flannel shirt. Green plaid flannel shirt. Used man's tuxedo shirt.

Then she saw it. At the very back of the closet, collecting lint, dust, and the smell of a Salvation Army store, was a depressingly cute baby doll dress. The outfit had been a gift from her misguided father the previous Christmas, and that morning he'd asked, no, *begged* her to wear it to Thanksgiving dinner.

Nina pulled the dress off the hanger and slipped it on over the boxers and T-shirt she slept in. Were those bluebells on the sleeves? Nina held a sleeve to her face. Yes, definitely bluebells. And the rest of the dress was covered with some undefinable flower pattern.

Nina punched a button on her CD player, filling the room with the sound of the Red Hot Chili Peppers. She grabbed a Lucky Strike from the half-empty pack on her desk and stuck it, unlit, into her mouth. Then she turned to her full-length mirror.

Just as Nina had feared, she was a dead ringer for Laura Ingalls in *Little House on the Prairie*. She was Pa's favorite half-pint in a dress that would make prairie dogs run for cover. "I guess this is what people call family loyalty," she muttered.

Normally Nina didn't worry about pleasing the family units. Especially her older sister, Princess Claire. But Claire hadn't asked her to wear this dress, she reminded herself. Her dad had—in a tentative voice that had been, frankly, embarrassing.

Mr. Geiger was bringing someone to Thanksgiving dinner. A woman someone. Since Nina and Claire's mother had died five years earlier, Mr. Geiger had been alone. Over the last couple of months, Nina had thought a lot about her father's extended state of singlehood. She hated to think of him twenty years down the road, tottering around some old-age home, bitter and alone. But the news that he'd actually met a woman—all on his own—had come as a major shock.

Sarah Mendel. Nina repeated the mystery woman's name in her mind, wondering what she was like. She wasn't from Chatham Island, the small island off the coast of Maine where Nina and Claire, along with the rest of their friends, had grown up. The island had only about three hundred year-round residents, so there was no way that any single, eligible woman would have escaped Nina's notice.

Unless the woman, of course, was totally wrong for Mr. Geiger. For instance, if she was into honky-tonks and country music, she would *not* be compatible with Nina's dad. Or if she'd

17

been holed up in one of the island's more isolated houses for the last fifteen years, doing nothing but trying to teach her nine million cats to do dog tricks. Nina thought for another moment, then smiled. Or if this Sarah Mendel had a big goiter on the side her neck. In Nina's opinion, goiters weren't great for romance.

The sound of someone pounding on the door joined the blaring Chili Peppers. "Just a second!" Nina yelled over the music.

She pulled off the dress. No way was she going to let anyone see her in the baby doll before she absolutely had to. The person who was pounding rattled the doorknob impatiently. *Claire*, Nina thought. *What does the Princess of Darkness want this early in the morning?*

Nina turned the deadbolt. She'd installed the lock on her door before her scumbag uncle and living-in-a-dream-world aunt had come to visit a couple of months earlier. She didn't technically need it anymore. But she liked it.

Nina opened the door a crack. "What do you want?" she asked.

Claire put her hands over her ears. "Turn that down!" she shouted.

Nina smiled serenely, then crossed the room to her stereo. She cranked the volume knob up to ten, just to annoy Claire, then pressed pause.

She went back to the door. As usual, Claire looked as if she'd just stepped out of a magazine. She'd obviously taken a shower, and her long, dark hair was shining. And even in old jeans and a Gap work shirt, the sight of Claire's body could cause a five-car highway pileup. When would her breasts have the decency to sag—just a little?

"I repeat, what do you want?" Nina stood in the doorway in case Claire had any ideas about coming into Nina's room.

"You don't have to stand there like a rabid watchdog, Nina. I'm about as interested in entering your room as I am in pitching a tent in Bosnia."

Nina rolled her eyes. It wasn't even noon, and Claire had scored the first point of the day. She made a mental note to get in a good zinger during dinner. "Did you come down here just to flatter me, or do you need help moving your coffin, Claire?"

Claire arched a perfectly plucked eyebrow. "Nina, Nina, Nina," she said with a sigh. "Your vampire jokes are getting lamer and lamer. I think dating my old boyfriend is turning your brain to mush."

Nina grimaced. As secure as she felt in her relationship with Benjamin, she didn't like to be reminded that he'd spent over a year being in love with her annoyingly beautiful sister. "Get to the point, Claire. Unlike you, I have things to do. It's called a life—you might want to get one of your own."

"The point *is*, Dad's bringing some bimbo to dinner," Claire said.

Nina decided to let the bimbo remark pass

19

for the moment. After all, she had her own doubts about this Sarah Mendel woman. "So I've been told. Dad made me promise to dress up like a reject from a Laura Ashley catalog."

"What should we do?"

"Do?" Nina asked blankly.

Claire rolled her eyes. "If we don't like her, we'll need a solid plan to get rid of her. Something along the lines of you just being yourself should do the trick."

Nina was about to shoot back that they could let the woman know that Claire drank a pint of blood for breakfast, but she stopped herself. The remark about her vampire jokes had stung. Instead, Nina decided to take the always-effective mature route. Seeing Nina act in a semirational manner always threw Claire for a loop.

"Claire, I think we should give Sarah every benefit of the doubt. If Dad enjoys her company, I'm sure we will, too."

For a split second Claire looked surprised. Then she shrugged casually. "I didn't realize you two were on a first-name basis."

Nina went in for the kill. Even Claire was capable of feeling guilt—occasionally. "Don't you want Dad to be happy? Or are you too selfish to think about the joy this new love is bringing to his lonely heart?"

Claire frowned, almost imperceptibly. "I never thought I'd see the day when *you* would sound like a bad Hallmark card."

Nina grinned. "Lessons from Zoey. She can teach anybody how to talk like a sap."

Claire shook her head, as if she couldn't believe that Nina was related to her. The expression on her face was one Nina had seen many times. "Just don't come crying to me if you don't like *Sarah*."

Claire climbed the stairs to her third-floor bedroom, still thinking about what a pain Nina could be. Claire had seen right through Nina's childish guilt ploy. Of course, Claire was an expert on ploys. She found manipulation to be a useful and necessary tool in life, and she used it often.

In her room, Claire pulled a heavy sweater over her head. She grabbed her journal and crossed to the ladder that led to the widow's walk on the roof, directly over her bedroom. As she had done thousands of times over the last seventeen years, Claire pushed open the trapdoor in her ceiling with one hand, then hoisted herself onto the roof.

Outside, the air was crisp and cold. Claire walked to the edge of the widow's walk and gazed out over the tiny town of North Harbor. The streets were empty, which wasn't unusual. Feeling restless, Claire turned her head to look out over the Atlantic Ocean. Even the sea was calm that day. Could life get more boring?

Since she and Jake had broken up, her life had taken a depressing turn toward the mundane.

She'd thought things were going to pick up when she'd met a guy on the Internet, but that situation had ended in disaster.

Claire still felt a pang as she remembered Sean. They'd talked every day for weeks, computer to computer. Claire had told Sean things about herself that she'd never told anyone. Not even Benjamin, who probably knew her better than anyone else. But when they'd finally met, Sean's outside hadn't been as appealing as his inside. Claire knew her reaction to Sean had been superficial, but what could she do? She was what she was, and she probably always would be. Since then, no one had sparked her romantic interest.

Claire sat down and propped her journal open on her knees.

November 28, Thanksgiving

Sun climbing high in a bright blue sky. A day the Pilgrims would have loved, no doubt. Personally, I wish there were a storm. I'd like to see the kind of storm that inspired the name for *The Tempest.*

Even some light snow would do.

It snowed on the Thanksgiving before my mother died. I remember, because Nina and I went out and tried to make a snowman. Actually, a snowwoman. We got along a lot better back then.

Now my father has a new girlfriend. She can't possibly measure up to my mother. No one could. Still, I'm glad my father's met someone he likes. I guess. But why has he kept her a secret till now? He just sprang this on me this morning.

"Oh, Claire," he said, staring at his newspaper, "I've been dating a *woman who works at the bank. She and her son are coming for dinner."*

So now I've got to deal with this new facet of my father's life. It turns out he's human after all. Who would have guessed it?

Claire shut the journal and put the cap back on her pen. She felt a slight sense of satisfaction over the fact that Nina didn't know about the son. She'd overheard her father asking Nina to wear the hideous baby doll instead of her usual army fatigues and flannel. He'd neglected to mention Aaron Mendel, Sarah's seventeen-year-old son, who was visiting from Connecticut.

Yes, the sight of some geeky prep-school kid would definitely catch Nina off guard. Claire couldn't wait to see the shock on her sister's face. Knowing Nina, the prospect of an annoying stepbrother would put a damper on her newly romantic self.

As usual, Claire had the upper hand. Just the way she liked it.

Aisha

Thanksgiving usually involves my mom running around the inn like an African-American version of Martha Stewart. She decorates the entire downstairs of our family's bed and breakfast with dried gourds, pumpkins, and petrified corncobs. Then she makes this really huge, ridiculously elaborate meal. I'm always stuck peeling potatoes and chopping parsley while Dad and Kalif watch football games.

This year my mom invited Christopher to spend the day with us, so he'll probably be in

on the football watching. Having
Christopher at the table for
Thanksgiving will be weird,
sort of like he's part of the
family or something.

I'm not sure how I feel
about that. No, wait a second. A
word just sprang to mind:
thankful.

Christopher

Right now I'm thankful for lots of stuff. I'm thankful for Aisha, and not just because she has the softest lips I've ever kissed. She also saved my butt big-time when she kept me from screwing up life by taking a shot at a punk skinhead who beat the crap out of me.

And I'm not spending another Thanksgiving in the inner city with my very dysfunctional family, which is also good. Instead, I'm going to the Grays'. I guess I have to wear a tie and probably a suit jacket. Mrs. Gray has a tendency to make a big production out of things. I pretend to think her attitude is kind of silly,

BUT THE TRUTH IS, I LIKE MRS. GRAY'S WAY OF DOING THINGS.

I HOPE THAT AFTER DINNER AISHA AND I CAN GET IN SOME MAJOR MAKE-OUT TIME. SINCE I DECIDED TO GIVE UP THE GIRLS I SOMETIMES SAW ON THE SIDE, I'VE BEEN CRAVING MORE OF AISHA'S, UH, AFFECTION. IF YOU KNOW WHAT I MEAN.

Two

Christopher Shupe wiped a hand covered with mashed potatoes on the front of his apron. It wasn't even one o'clock, and he was already covered in a mixture of sweat and the makings of Thanksgiving dinner.

Since moving to Chatham Island, Christopher had worked a medley of part-time jobs. He delivered papers every morning at four, did odd jobs around his apartment house and the Grays' bed-and-breakfast, and even worked at the high school in Weymouth. But his steadiest supply of cash came from Passmores', the restaurant Zoey and Benjamin's parents owned in North Harbor. He still had a couple more hours of cooking before he could shower, change, and climb the hill to Aisha's.

Over the last few months, Aisha Gray had become the most important person in his life. He laughed out loud as he remembered how much resistance Aisha had put up when he'd first asked her out. She'd insisted that the only reason he was interested in her was because, aside from Aisha's fourteen-year-old brother, Kalif, she and Christopher were the only two African-American teenagers on Chatham Island. But Christopher had poured on the charm until even stubborn Aisha couldn't deny the attraction between them.

When they'd first started going out, he'd managed to screw things up pretty badly. He'd dated other girls on the side, which had almost destroyed their relationship. But when he'd finally decided to be a one-woman man, she'd given him a second chance. Thank God.

Mr. Passmore appeared in the kitchen's swinging door. "Yo, Christopher, how's it going back here?"

Christopher gestured toward the counter covered with pots and pans. "I could use some help, to tell you the truth."

Mr. Passmore nodded, grabbing an apron from a hook on the wall. He stuck his ponytail down the back of his shirt and stood next to Christopher at the counter. "Zoey just got here, so she's helping Darla with the bourgeois place settings we put out for holidays."

"Cool." Christopher went on mashing potatoes.

After a few minutes he noticed that Mr. Passmore was just standing motionless, staring into space. "Uh, Mr. P.? Anyone home?"

Zoey's dad blinked quickly several times, as if to bring himself back to planet Earth. "Sorry, Christopher. I guess I've got something on my mind."

Christopher turned his attention to the cranberry sauce, cursing himself. Now that he'd opened his big mouth, he was faced with a

30

dilemma. Should he ask Mr. Passmore, an adult, if he wanted to confide what was wrong? Or should he keep silent and assume that the aging hippie could deal on his own with whatever was bothering him?

"Mind if I get your opinion on something, Christopher?" Mr. Passmore asked, deciding the question.

"Sure. Just think of me as a bartender in a cook's uniform."

The older man smiled, but he still looked as if he were a million miles away. "Well, I've planned a sort of surprise for Zoey and her mom, and I'm not sure they're going to be thrilled with it."

"Sounds interesting," Christopher said. He stirred the cranberries.

"Yeah, well, I've invited Lara McAvoy, my other daughter, to Thanksgiving dinner."

Christopher let out a low whistle. This was big. "And they don't know about it, huh?"

"Benjamin does. I told him this morning. But I made him promise to keep quiet. I wanted Zoey and Darla to hear the news from me." Mr. Passmore bit his lip and stared at the roast turkey that he'd just taken out of the oven.

"Maybe they'll be excited," Christopher said, although he seriously doubted that Zoey would be thrilled with the news. "You know, getting to know a whole new relative and all."

Mr. Passmore was silent for a moment, then his face relaxed. "You know what, Christopher?"

31

"What?"

"You're absolutely right. Thanksgiving is a day for family. Why shouldn't Zoey and Darla be happy to include Lara in our celebration?"

"Yeah, why not?" Christopher said.

Mr. Passmore reached behind him and turned on the cassette player he kept at the restaurant. The sounds of the Grateful Dead filtered through the kitchen. Since Jerry Garcia had died, Mr. Passmore had been listening to the Dead more than ever.

Mr. Passmore moved in time to the music, humming softly. "This is going to be the best Thanksgiving ever, Christopher. I can feel it."

"What?" Zoey yelped. She stared at her father in horror.

"You're kidding," Mrs. Passmore said flatly. She was also staring at Zoey's father in utter dismay.

Zoey and her mother had been putting the finishing touches on the fancy place settings they used for holiday meals at the restaurant when Mr. Passmore had glided into the dining room humming along with a Dead tune. Then he'd casually announced that he'd invited his love child, Lara, to the Thanksgiving dinner that the Passmores would have at their house later that evening, after the restaurant closed.

Mr. Passmore smiled, but Zoey could tell that their reaction to his bombshell had made him a little nervous. "We can't pretend she doesn't exist," he said. "She's family."

Mrs. Passmore raised an eyebrow. "She's not *my* family."

"Dad, she's, like, a total druggie," Zoey said. The forks she'd been holding dangled forgotten at her side. "She'll probably steal from us."

Mr. Passmore frowned. "Zoey, this is your sister we're talking about."

"My *half* sister." Zoey set the forks down on a table and sank into a chair.

"Benjamin didn't think it was a bad idea," Mr. Passmore said. He glanced from Zoey to Mrs. Passmore, as if looking for an ally.

"Benjamin *knew* about this? And he didn't *tell* me?" Zoey yelled.

She flinched as her father patted her on the head. "I thought I should tell you myself."

Mrs. Passmore cleared her throat. "Zoey, your dad is right. Lara is alone. We should be generous enough to invite her to join us for Thanksgiving."

With both parents on the same side, there was no way to win this battle. Lara McAvoy was coming to dinner.

Zoey sighed. "At least it's just one day."

Fifteen minutes later, Zoey turned off Dock Street and headed up South Street toward home, where she planned to confront her lousy brother. She couldn't believe that he'd let her go on and on like an idiot that morning. After Lucas had taken off, she'd eaten two bowls of Cheerios, talking between mouthfuls about how great it was that life was back to normal.

Zoey jogged up the walkway that led to the Passmores' front door. In her mind she rehearsed the scathing lecture she was going to lay on Benjamin.

"Benjamin!" Zoey slammed the front door and ripped off her Lands End parka.

Her brother didn't answer, but Zoey heard music blasting from his room. An opera. Since Benjamin had lost his sight several years before, he'd developed a taste for almost every type of music. Lately he'd been trying to get into opera.

She pushed open his bedroom door without bothering to knock. "Benjamin, how could you let Dad ambush me like that?"

"Oh, uh, hi, Zoey," Nina said. She was lying next to Benjamin on his bed.

Nina and Benjamin were tangled together, as if they'd been playing a game of Twister that had suddenly gone out of control. One of Nina's hands was buried in Benjamin's thick, dark hair, and his ever-present sunglasses were askew. Nina's olive skin was flushed, and her long brown hair was even more disarrayed than usual.

Zoey felt a blush rise to her cheeks as she stared at her best friend. "Hi, Nina. Uh, sorry to interrupt, but I need to talk to Benjamin."

Benjamin readjusted the black Ray-Bans he always wore and fixed an unseeing gaze in Zoey's direction. With one hand he groped for the remote control to his stereo. When he found it, he turned down the volume of the opera. "Shoot, Zoey. Nina was just about to tie me up and ravish me. You ruined a very romantic moment."

Zoey rolled her eyes, a gesture that was lost on Benjamin, but not on Nina, who hopped up from the bed. "I should be going anyway. I have to make myself into Barbie for Dad's new girlfriend."

Zoey momentarily forgot about the Lara McAvoy crisis. "Since when does your dad have a girlfriend?"

Nina shrugged, then sat down next to Benjamin and shoved her feet into her shoes. "Got me. He just sprang it on me this morning. She's coming to dinner."

"Jeez! What's the deal with surprise dinner guests today?" Zoey said.

Nina finished lacing up her Doc Martens. "That's my cue to leave."

"Not so fast, Nina." Zoey stood in the doorway, blocking Nina's exit. "Did Benjamin tell you that Lara's coming here for dinner?"

"Just now, Zo, I swear. I got here a little while ago, and he was like, 'So, Nina, my crazy half sister's showing up for turkey day.'"

"Do you have anything to say for yourself, Benjamin?" Zoey demanded.

"Sensing an opportunity to flee, the heroine snuck out of the tension-filled bedroom," Nina interjected in a dramatic voice. She slipped past Zoey and headed toward the front door.

"See you guys later," she called. Zoey heard the door bang shut behind her.

Benjamin turned off the opera. "Zoey, be rational. You can't blame Dad for wanting to get to know his daughter."

Zoey walked farther into the room and sat down at Benjamin's desk. She ran her fingers over the keyboard of her brother's computer. "None of this would be happening if you and Nina hadn't played Sherlock Holmes and Dr. Watson."

After Mr. Passmore had informed Zoey and Benjamin that they had a mysterious half sister, Benjamin had taken it upon himself to hunt her down. He'd found that she lived in Weymouth, the small coastal town across the bay from Chatham Island.

Benjamin had gotten Nina to lead him around town, following Lara and her sleazy boyfriend. By the end of the night, the boyfriend had given Benjamin a few choice punches, and Benjamin had formally introduced himself to Lara McAvoy. Since then, neither Zoey nor Benjamin had talked to her.

"I was curious to meet her, Zoey," Benjamin said in a serious voice. "Aren't you?"

Zoey didn't answer right away. She looked around her brother's room, glancing for the millionth time at the posters he'd hung upside down as a kind of blind in-joke. Zoey couldn't imagine what life would be like without her brother.

What would it be like to have a sister as well? Would they have stuff in common? Maybe they'd have an instant connection, like the twins separated at birth and reunited after thirty years that she'd seen on one of the daytime talk shows.

But Zoey doubted that any kind of psychic bond existed. Nina had described Lara as a potentially attractive girl who favored trashy clothes and heavy makeup. But Lara was her sister, and Zoey would be lying if she said she wasn't even curious about her.

"Yes, Benjamin," she admitted. "I am curious. But why does she have to ruin our Thanksgiving? I mean, what's wrong with Sunday brunch in Weymouth? Why does she have to come *here?*"

"Why not?" Benjamin asked, answering her question with a question.

"Well, Mom doesn't like the idea, either," Zoey said defensively.

"Mom's a big girl. She can take care of herself," Benjamin said.

Zoey stared at Europe on the world map tacked upside down on Benjamin's wall. Her father had met Lara's mother during a backpacking trip in Europe. Even though Jeff Passmore was in love with Zoey's mother at the time, he'd had an affair. Lara was the unknown result.

Much to Zoey's disgust, the soap opera didn't stop there. Before Jeff Passmore had left for Europe, Darla had become pregnant—with Benjamin. At least, that's what the story was. At the same time that Mr. Passmore had been fooling around, Mrs. Passmore had been having an affair with Fred McRoyan, Jake's dad.

Zoey studied Benjamin's face, suddenly understanding why he was so interested in spending time with Lara. "You're still worried that Jake's dad is your real father, aren't you?" she asked.

"Don't be stupid, Zoey," he said, clicking his CD player back on.

Zoey walked over to the stereo and switched off the power. "Benjamin, we're not done talking about this."

"There's nothing to say," Benjamin said. "We'll just have to see how things go. Maybe Lara will surprise you."

Zoey thought back to Nina's description of Lara and her sleazy boyfriend, whom Nina had called 'Mr. Hair'. "I doubt it."

She turned the stereo back on and quietly left the room. As she headed upstairs for her second hot shower of the day, Zoey had the sinking feeling that everything was about to change. And not for the better.

Three

At 2:55 P.M. Nina squinted at herself in the bathroom mirror. As she'd expected, there was yet another clump of mascara on her eyelashes. Holding the goopy applicator in one hand, she gave the instrument the finger with the other. Why did they call these things *wands?* Wands were for magic and fairy godmothers. Mascara applicators had probably originated as some form of ancient Chinese torture.

"Are you almost done in there?" Claire yelled, banging on the bathroom door.

"Not all of us wake up looking like Cindy Crawford," Nina called back. "It takes me some time to get that plastic, silicone-enhanced effect."

Nina tossed both the tube of mascara and the wand in the trash. She took a last look at herself in the baby doll dress and stuck out her tongue at her image. She looked exactly like Tammy Faye Bakker.

Nina shut the lid on the toilet and sat down for a few minutes. She didn't want Claire to think she'd hurried for her sake.

"Is she here yet?" Nina asked when she opened the door.

Claire put on her most bored expression. "How should I know?"

"You know those two big senses, sight and hearing? They kind of, like, alert you as to whether or not a certain person has or has not arrived for dinner."

Claire sneered, her version of a smile. "You look like Tammy Faye Bakker."

Leave it to Claire to zero in on an insecurity and slap you in the face with it, Nina thought. Claire had probably never had to deal with an insidious clump of mascara. But her sister locked herself in the bathroom before Nina could think of a snappy comeback.

Downstairs, the Geigers' housekeeper, Janelle, was moving around the kitchen like Julia Child on speed. Nina's mouth watered at the sight of sweet potatoes topped with marshmallows. She'd always thought Janelle's sweet potatoes were the most redeeming aspect of Thanksgiving.

"Can I do anything?" Nina asked, sidestepping Janelle as the housekeeper barreled across the kitchen with a bowl of mashed turnips (in Nina's opinion, the *least* redeeming aspect of Thanksgiving).

"Ayuh," Janelle said. She was one of the few people Nina knew who actually used that old Maine word in regular conversation. "Go say hello to Ms. Mendel and her son."

Nina frowned at this new piece of information. Her dad hadn't mentioned anything about a kid. "Her son?" Nina asked, in case she'd heard wrong.

"That's what I said." Janelle nudged Nina away from the oven and bent down with a meat thermometer in her hand.

Nina stepped through the kitchen's swinging door and entered the dining room. She wasn't quite ready to confront this new person in her father's life, and she wanted to prepare herself for the kid. In fact, she didn't know if the term *kid* applied. Maybe he was a grown man, or just a little baby.

Nina hoped he wasn't a baby. Drool and dirty diapers weren't appetizing additions to Thanksgiving dinner. Although an infant would be preferable to some bratty little kid who thought loud belching was a form of entertainment.

From inside the living room, Nina heard a low, husky laugh. The sound was distinctly different from her father's restrained chuckle. At least the son wasn't a baby. Or a little kid. That laugh had definitely been postpuberty. Nina walked out of the dining room, pasting her phony nice-to-meet-you-smile on her face.

At the door of the living room, Nina did a double take. Her father was sitting on the couch, smiling in a way that made Nina wonder if he'd taken one too many Geritols.

Burke Geiger was always pleasant and charming. He always grinned at appropriate moments in any social setting. But usually his

41

smile didn't quite reach his eyes. He was the kind of man who made middle-aged married women shake their heads sadly. "Poor Burke," they'd say. "He hasn't been the same since his wife died."

But at the moment, Nina's father looked as if he had a lighthouse inside his head. He was beaming, yes, *beaming*, at the petite woman who looked as if she were glued to his side. The couple looked like one of those keep-in-touch ads for a long-distance phone company.

The shock of seeing her father look like an infatuated teenager almost made her forget to investigate the source of the low, husky laugh. Almost, but not quite.

Her gaze moved to the overstuffed armchair next to the couch. Lounging comfortably in the chair was one of the best-looking guys Nina had ever seen. The Son. Why hadn't Janelle mentioned that he was a dead ringer for Brad Pitt? Nina stood awkwardly, waiting for one of them to notice she was there.

"Nina!" her father boomed suddenly. "You're here."

"Yep. Pantyhose and all," she responded.

Nina noticed that when her father stood up, he kept hold of Sarah Mendel's hand. Or was it the other way around? Nina wasn't sure.

"I'd like to introduce you to Sarah Mendel and her son, Aaron," Mr. Geiger said, as if he were offering her tickets to Nirvana's sold-out last concert.

"Nina, I'm just pleased as punch to meet you," Sarah Mendel chirped, standing up next to Nina's father.

"Uh, likewise," Nina answered.

Beside Sarah Mendel, Nina felt like Big Bird. The woman was tiny. She had to be five feet at the most, Nina assessed. And when Nina shook her hand, she was seriously afraid that the woman's bones were going to shatter in her grip.

"And this is Aaron," her father said. He swung an arm around Aaron's shoulders as if the guy were his long-lost son.

"Hi, Nina. Great to meet you."

"Uh, likewise," she squeaked. Was there an echo, or was that her sounding like an idiot?

Nina was one hundred percent in love with Benjamin. But a cute guy was a cute guy. And Aaron Mendel certainly fell into the cute guy category.

"Where's Claire?" Mr. Geiger asked. He'd reclaimed Sarah's hand and was clinging to it as if she were a life raft in shark-infested waters.

"Upstairs," Nina said. For the sake of propriety, she didn't add that her sister was probably busy kicking a puppy or devouring human flesh.

"No, she's not," Claire said from the doorway. "She's right here."

Claire positioned herself across the table from Aaron Mendel. He was cute, bordering on being the best-looking guy she had ever seen.

Something stirred in Claire, and she recognized it as the beginnings of physical attraction. But if Aaron was even half as sweet and cheery as his mother, Claire was sure the sensation would die before she felt moved to do anything about it.

Sarah Mendel, who insisted on being called by her first name, was the kind of woman who probably baked chocolate chip cookies and made needlepoint throw-pillow covers in her spare time. And she liked to talk.

In the last ten minutes, Claire had learned that two months earlier Sarah had moved from New York, where, according to her, people really *are* rude and inconsiderate, to Maine, where people are "just lovely." Sarah had gone on to inform the group how she and Mr. Geiger had met (by means of a fax machine at the bank) and how Mr. Geiger had first asked her out (blushing and stammering and looking as if he were about to have a heart attack). Claire was thankful Nina had stopped the conversation before Sarah launched into a detailed description of the couple's first kiss.

Sarah had also explained, in one very long run-on sentence, that the pipes in her Weymouth apartment had burst, so she'd decided to stay temporarily at the Grays' B&B. "Where I can be closer to Burke," she'd said with a saccharine smile.

The only items of Sarah Mendel's background that Claire had found the least bit interesting were those having to do with Aaron. He was a senior at a boarding school in Connecticut, where he was at the top of his class. Although his school was on break from Thanksgiving until the beginning of January, he'd be leaving Maine in a few days to go skiing with his father.

While his mother divulged his life story, Aaron had sat quietly, a tolerant smile on his face. Since they'd come into the dining room, his expression hadn't changed.

Just as Nina reached across the table for the sweet potatoes, Sarah piped up yet again. "Shall we say grace?"

Nina snatched her hand back into her lap and glanced at Claire. Claire shrugged slightly.

Mr. Geiger set down his fork. "Oh, yes, of course. Wonderful idea, Sarah."

Sarah rested a hand on Mr. Geiger's arm. "Why don't we go around the table and each say what we're thankful for this year?"

Claire wanted to laugh, but managed to look expectant. She heard a half-snort from Nina, who picked up her water glass and started chugging.

"Burke, why don't you begin?" Sarah continued.

Mr. Geiger's face was turning a pale shade of pink, but he cleared his throat purposefully. "Ah, yes, let's see now. Well, I'm thankful to have my family together, happy and healthy. . . ."

Except for Mom, Claire thought. A lump rose in her throat, and a single tear threatened to escape. Claire bit the inside of her cheek and masked her face with a pleasantly indifferent smile.

"And I especially want to give thanks for Sarah's entrance into my life. For the first time in years, I feel alive again." Mr. Geiger finished his prayer and looked expectantly at Sarah.

Claire didn't listen to Sarah's speech. She was digesting the fact that her father seemed to have acquired cornball syndrome overnight.

Nina looked as if she wanted to crawl under the table. For once, Claire felt sympathetic. The Geigers weren't known for their sentimentality.

"Aaron, why don't you go next?" Sarah suggested. "You're an old pro at this."

Aaron smiled at his mother, then winked at Claire. "I'm thankful for my many blessings," he said simply. "And I hope that my mother enjoys having her loving son around for the holiday."

Aaron's wink affected Claire in the oddest manner. Her heart seemed to expand, and she experienced a sense of titillating anticipation.

"She does," Sarah assured him. "Claire, your turn."

Claire racked her brain trying to think of something to say. Finally she took a deep breath. "I'm thankful that we're all here together. And I'm thankful that my dad seems so happy."

It was the most gratitude she'd ever expressed at one time, but she thought she'd pulled it off pretty well. Aaron was staring at her. Claire held his gaze for several seconds, then dropped her eyes.

"Nina?" Mr. Geiger prompted. Now that his

turn was over, he seemed to be enjoying the spectacle of his daughters being totally embarrassed.

Nina bit her lip, then smiled triumphantly. "Ditto."

Sarah looked disappointed. Aaron looked mildly amused. Mr. Geiger looked exasperated.

"Jeez, Nina, I never thought I'd see you at a loss for words," Claire said.

Nina took another gulp of ice water. "Can I have the sweet potatoes, please?"

Claire handed her sister the dish, studying Aaron out of the corner of her eye. He was grinning blandly at her father. *Okay, Aaron Mendel*, Claire thought. *Let the games begin*.

The dinner conversation had consisted largely of Mr. Geiger and Sarah Mendel gazing at each other and laughing at inside jokes. Nina had said all the wrong things. Aaron had said all the right things. Claire had mostly been silent.

Nina slipped into the kitchen and picked up the phone. Ever since the grace session, she'd felt on the brink of totally losing it. Too much goodwill and cheer made her light-headed.

"Hey, it's me," Nina said when she heard Zoey's voice.

"Aren't you in the middle of your Thanksgiving?" Zoey sounded suspicious, probably because Nina was whispering.

"Digestion break," Nina explained.

"So what do you think of her?" Zoey asked.

47

"I don't know. But my dad is mooning over her like he's fifteen."

"What does she look like?"

"I think she's a dwarf. Or a midget. I never could get those two straight. Maybe the anatomically correct term is *munchkin*."

"Is she nice?" Zoey asked.

"Does the name *June Cleaver* ring a bell? How about *Carol Brady*?"

"Nina, I'm serious."

"So am I."

"Well, there's nothing wrong with June or Carol. After all, *Leave It to Beaver* and *The Brady Bunch* are still in syndication."

"So are *Charles in Charge* and *Who's the Boss?* Syndication means nothing."

"Nina, go eat pumpkin pie. We'll talk later."

"The pie can wait. You have to come over. Now."

"Why?"

"I want your opinion of this Sarah woman. I can't decide if I like her or hate her."

Nina heard Zoey's sigh. "You might as well decide to like her, then."

"Come on, Zoey. You can meet her son."

"She's got a kid? What's he like?"

Nina pictured Aaron. Too bad that pretty face was wasted on such a do-gooder personality. In her mind, good looks were neutralized by an uninteresting brain. "You can see for yourself if you come over."

Zoey paused. "Fine. On one condition."

"What?"

"You'll come to our house afterward and help me face the half sister from hell."

Nina appreciated any excuse to see Benjamin. "Deal."

Zoey stamped her feet as she waited for Nina to answer the door. The temperature had dropped about fifteen degrees since she'd been out earlier, and the wind felt as if it were blowing a hundred miles an hour. The wool skirt Zoey had changed into ended above her knees, and her white tights provided very little protection against the cold.

Finally Nina flung the door open. "Thank goodness you're here," she whispered loudly.

"Is it that bad?" Zoey asked, pulling her Patagonian jacket off over her head.

Nina rolled her eyes. "Everyone's so damn happy, I could puke."

"Happy is a bad thing?" Zoey opened the front hall closet and shoved her jacket onto a hanger. Then she stuffed her hands into the pockets of Claire's old rabbit-fur jacket to get the feeling back. "Ew. I think your sister has tissues from, like, 1987 in these pockets," she said.

Nina pulled nervously at the bodice of her baby doll dress. "Come upstairs with me for a few minutes. I need a cigarette."

Zoey sighed with exasperation. Nina had a perpetual habit of sucking on unlit Lucky Strikes. Her dad (not to mention her friends) disapproved, but since there was nothing strictly unhealthy about simply holding a cigarette, he didn't out-and-out forbid Nina to do it.

"Let me get a look at Sarah first," Zoey whispered.

"Okay. They're all in there." Nina gestured toward the living room. "But don't let them see you yet. Sarah will invite you in for a sing-along around the piano."

"Nina, you guys don't have a piano," Zoey reminded her.

"Just keep it quiet. I need a break from the festivities."

Zoey crept to the entrance of the living room. Mr. Geiger and Claire had their backs to her, but she had a perfect view of Sarah Mendel and her son.

Zoey felt her eyeballs attempt to jump out of their sockets as she stared at the guy sitting on the Geigers' couch. He was the best-looking guy Zoey had ever seen. With longish, wavy dark hair and full red lips, the guy looked like a spokesmodel for Obsession cologne.

He glanced up and caught Zoey's eye. "Hi," he mouthed.

She gasped, feeling blood rush to her cheeks. What should she do? She couldn't just stand there gaping like a fish. But if she said something at this point, it would seem as though she'd been trying to spy. Of course, she *had* been trying to spy.

The guy's mouth curved in the merest hint of a smile, then he turned his gaze to Mr.

Geiger. Zoey's heart started to beat again, and she stepped back into the front hall.

"Very funny," Zoey hissed to Nina, jerking her head in the direction of the living room.

"What?" Nina asked innocently.

"You left out a few details about the son."

"Who, *moi?*" Nina grinned and walked to the staircase.

In Nina's room, Zoey flopped on the bed, which was covered with clothes and CDs.

"Nina, the most beautiful guy ever to set foot on Chatham Island is sitting in your living room."

Nina shrugged. "He's cute, yes. But boring."

"Nina, you've known him for all of two hours. You couldn't possibly know whether or not he's boring."

"Whatever." Nina grabbed the huge leather bag she used for a purse and started to rummage through it. "Did you get a good look at Sarah?"

"She is *not* a dwarf. She's very pretty."

"Aha!" Nina pulled a crumpled pack of Lucky Strikes from her bag and removed a mangled-looking cigarette from it. "She made us say grace before dinner."

"Really?"

"Yep. And I mean *all* of us. We had to go around the table and take turns. The whole experience was incredibly traumatic."

Zoey was thinking about the smile that Sarah Mendel's son had given her. Was *angelic* a word that applied to teenage boys?

"Tell me his name."

"I assume you're talking about Aaron." Nina sucked on the cigarette, then exhaled loudly.

"Aaron . . . ," Zoey repeated slowly. "What's his deal?"

"His parents divorced when he was young. He used to live with his mom, but now he goes to some fancy-schmancy boarding school. He spends weekends at his dad's in Connecticut."

"I suppose he's already fallen madly in love with Claire."

"Probably." Nina took another imaginary puff.

Zoey felt strangely deflated. "Well, I guess we should go down there."

"They can wait."

"Come on, Nina. We don't have all that long before we have to go over to my house."

"Okay, okay." Nina tossed the cigarette in her trash can. "By the way, is Lucas coming to dinner at your house?"

Nina's voice reached Zoey from far away. She was wondering what color eyes Aaron Mendel had.

"Lucas?" she said absently.

"Lucas Cabral? Your boyfriend?"

Zoey shook her head from side to side, forcing herself to conjure up a mental image of Lucas. He was at least as good-looking as Aaron, she reminded herself. In a different way.

"Oh, yeah. I mean, no. I mean, I think he's coming over later."

Nina had her hand on the doorknob. "Zo, are you all right?"

"Sure. Why?"

"You seem kind of out of it. I thought you might still be upset that Lara's dining *chez* Passmore tonight."

Zoey blinked. She'd totally forgotten that Lara McAvoy existed. "I don't want to think about that girl until I have to," she said, finally rising from the bed. "Let's go downstairs. I think I hear Sarah breaking into a round of 'Zippity Doo Dah'."

Nina banged her head against the wall. "Why me, Lord? Why me?"

Four

Aisha pursed her lips and carefully applied a coat of Passion Red. The dramatic color made her full mouth stand out against her smooth brown skin. She moved her head from side to side, studying the effect. Did her lips stand out in a good way, or did she look like a half-made-up circus clown? There was always a fine line where new lipstick was concerned.

Passion Red would have been a bit much for school, but Aisha decided the color was okay for a semiformal Thanksgiving dinner. She glanced at the little black dress she'd chosen for the occasion. Yeah, the lipstick would look a lot better next to black velvet than it did at the moment—she was still wearing a pair of her dad's old sweats and a Boston University T-shirt.

"Oh, yes, dahling," Aisha drawled to herself in the mirror. "You're looking absolutely fabulous. . . ."

She jumped away from the mirror when she heard a sharp rapping on her window. Christopher, of course.

He found his way to the window of her first-floor bedroom on a fairly regular basis. But usually Christopher arrived just before dawn, at the tail end of his paper route.

She opened the window, shivering as soon as the cold air hit her face. "Why didn't you just use the front door?" she asked.

"Hello to you, too." He put his hands on the sill and stuck his head inside.

Aisha put her warm hands on either side of his cold face. "Sorry. Hi."

Christopher grinned. "That's more like it." He pulled one of his gloves off with his teeth and placed his hand on the back of her neck. "And the reason I didn't go to the front door is because I knew I'd be immediately surrounded by Gray family members."

His low, sensuous voice, combined with the cold air, made goose bumps appear up and down her arms. "I thought you liked my family," she said.

"I do. But when they're around, I can't do this. . . ." Christopher's voice trailed off as he brought his lips close to hers.

Aisha didn't try to stop him, as she might have in the past. Now that she knew Christopher was being faithful to her, her doubts about him had vanished.

For the first few moments of the kiss, Christopher's lips were cold. As they grew warmer Aisha wrapped her arms around his shoulders. When Christopher pulled away, Aisha brushed her lips across his cheeks, his forehead, even his nose.

"I'll see you at the front door," Christopher said. She watched his retreating back as he made his way around the side of the house. For the millionth time, Aisha noted what a great butt her boyfriend had.

"They really don't come any finer than that," she announced to the worn teddy bear that was sitting on her dresser.

She looked outside once more to make sure he hadn't returned to the window, then stripped off the T-shirt and sweats. The black velvet dress fit as well now as it had in the dressing room at The Gap. Aisha slipped into her pumps and pivoted in front of the mirror.

She saw her own eyes widen as she caught a glimpse of her lips. "Uh-oh."

The Passion Red had come off her lips. The stuff was completely, totally gone. And Aisha had a feeling she knew exactly where to find it.

Christopher smoothed the paper wrapping around the pink roses he'd bought for Mrs. Gray. He'd parted with fifteen precious dollars for the flowers when he'd been on an errand for his landlady in Weymouth that morning.

Spending the money on the flowers meant that he'd have to give up a few luxuries, such as food, for the next several days if he wanted to stay on his strict budget. But he'd decided Mrs. Gray was worth the sacrifice. Several weeks earlier, she'd allowed Christopher to stay in the inn's nicest room, free of charge, while he'd recovered from the beating he'd gotten from the skinheads. While he'd been there, she'd given him access to a remote-control TV and a Jacuzzi and had pampered him with gourmet meals three times a day.

As soon as the door opened, Christopher could smell the turkey in the oven. His mouth watered as he held the roses out to Mrs. Gray. In a long blue dress and an apron that said Don't Mess with the Chef, Mrs. Gray looked like the quintessential mom. Christopher felt a flash of sadness at the thought of his own mother, who was probably eating a McDonald's cheese-burger for her Thanksgiving meal.

"Hello, Christopher," Mrs. Gray said. "We're glad you could join us."

Christopher stepped inside, holding the flowers out to Aisha's mom. "Thanks for inviting me. I've been looking forward to this all week."

Mrs. Gray took the flowers and inhaled deeply. "Oh, these are wonder—"

She broke off suddenly, staring at Christopher. He stared back, wondering if he'd suddenly grown an extra eyeball.

At that moment Aisha appeared behind her mother, looking incredibly sexy in a short, tight black dress. Christopher grew even more confused when Aisha came to a halt and slapped a hand across her mouth.

"What's wrong?" Christopher asked.

"Nothing, Christopher," Mrs. Gray said,

turning to glance at Aisha. "I just didn't realize you were partial to Passion Red."

Benjamin stood in front of his closet, deciding what to wear to Thanksgiving. His options were pretty limited, since most of his clothes were either white or black.

Still, there was always the bright plaid sport coat and polka-dot tie kept on a hook in the back of his closet. Benjamin wore the tie and jacket together when he felt like testing a stranger's reaction to his blindness. If the person laughed at his outfit, Benjamin decided he or she was probably pretty cool. But if the person whispered something sympathetic (as if Benjamin were deaf as well as blind), Benjamin knew to keep his guard up.

"Does Lara deserve the plaid jacket treatment?" he wondered aloud.

Benjamin reached for the jacket, then pulled out what he thought was a black blazer instead. The night was going to be pretty tough for Lara no matter what. And when he and Nina had tracked her down in Weymouth, Benjamin had learned that Lara wasn't the sharpest person around. Teasing her might amount to cruel and unusual punishment.

There was a rapping on his door just as he slipped into the blazer. He recognized his girl-friend's knock immediately. "Come in, Nina," he called.

"Hey, how'd you know it was me?" she asked.

Benjamin wiggled his eyebrows. "Simple. Your knock is always two light taps followed by a thump."

"It is?" Nina said. "What's Zoey's?"

"Several soft knuckle brushes, like she's worried that the sound of her knocking might disturb the neighbors."

"Amazing," Nina said. She slipped her arms around Benjamin's waist, and he pulled her close.

"Sorry we got interrupted earlier."

Nina kissed him quickly on the lips. "That's okay. I guess Zoey was kind of freaking out."

"And does that have something to do with why you're here now?" Benjamin asked.

"Yep. She called in the troops for reinforcement."

"Just like you called *her* for reinforcement, huh?"

"We women have to stick together."

"Just make sure you stick with me, too."

"Always." Nina hugged Benjamin close. Whenever he said one of those boyfriendish things to her, she thought her heart would burst with the sheer joy of being alive. *I guess that's what Dad must be feeling*, she realized suddenly.

"Let's go check out the action in the kitchen," Benjamin said. "They've already started the countdown to Lara's big entrance."

Lara McAvoy's outfit was much more conservative than Zoey had expected. She wore a stonewashed denim jumper over what looked like a unitard, and black cowboy boots.

"Zoey, meet Lara," Mr. Passmore said. "Lara, meet Zoey."

Mr. Passmore had gone to pick up Lara at the dock, and now there she was, standing in Zoey's front hall. As Lara unzipped her thin leather jacket, Zoey noted that the girl must have been freezing on the ferry. It was the nicest thought she'd had about her half sister since she'd learned of her existence.

Zoey forced the corners of her mouth upward. "Hi, Lara. It's nice to meet you."

"You're my sister," Lara said, looking Zoey up and down.

"Yeah, well, half sister." Lara's intense gaze made Zoey feel like a cross between a store mannequin and a piece of meat on the butcher's block.

Lara nodded to herself. "We have the same eyes."

"We do?" Zoey looked into Lara's light blue eyes.

She was right. Lara's eyes had the same dark lashes as Zoey's. And in the irises there were the same tiny flecks of darker blue. Lara really was her sister, whether Zoey liked it or not.

"I'm Darla," Mrs. Passmore said, coming out from the kitchen. "Jeff's wife."

Lara looked surprised when Mrs. Passmore offered her hand for Lara to shake. "Uh, hi. Where's the blind boy?"

"Stop it with the flattery," Benjamin said, emerging from behind Mrs. Passmore. "You can just call me Benjamin."

"Right," Mr. Passmore said in a cheerful voice. He looked so uncomfortable that Zoey felt sorry for him.

Nina appeared at Benjamin's side. "And I'm Nina. The family leech." Lara looked confused. "We met a few weeks ago."

"Oh, yeah. You're the girl who was trailing me the night of that party."

"Maybe we should all sit down," Benjamin said quickly.

Mr. Passmore smiled weakly. "Yes, let's all sit down. We've got a wonderful dinner in store."

Zoey was the last to enter the dining room. Lara had taken Zoey's usual place beside her mother. Zoey opened her mouth to say something but thought better of it.

It's just one night, Zoey, she told herself for the tenth time. *One very long night.*

Five

"Just sweet potatoes for me, Mrs. P.," Nina said. "This is my second dinner."

"And I'll be skipping dessert," Zoey said. "I had pumpkin pie at the Geigers'."

"Well, I'm starved," Benjamin said. "Pass me everything."

"Me too," Mr. Passmore said.

"Me three," Mrs. Passmore added. "I was smelling food all day down at the restaurant, but I didn't eat a bite."

Benjamin carefully took the bowl of stuffing that Zoey offered. He could sense that Lara was watching to see how a blind person managed at a dinner table, and he didn't want to appear at even more of a disadvantage than he was.

"So you all own a restaurant, huh?" Lara said.

Benjamin was surprised to hear her sudden, slightly harsh voice. Lara had hardly said a word since they'd sat down at the table; Mr. and Mrs. Passmore's awkward attempts to draw her into the conversation had been greeted with monosyllabic answers.

"Yeah, we've got a little place down by the

dock. I'll show it to you when I walk you to the water taxi later."

Interesting, Benjamin thought. His dad was shelling out the big bucks for a water taxi. He must have felt more guilty than anyone realized about not having had a relationship with Lara while she was growing up.

"Restaurants are cool. I'm a waitress."

Benjamin could tell that Lara was talking with food in her mouth. Apparently her mother had been a little lax in the table manners department.

"Tell us more about yourself, Lara," Mr. Passmore said. "Even though we've talked, I don't know much about how you spend your days."

"Not much to tell. Weymouth pretty much sucks."

"You're not into the *ye olde shoppe* scene, huh?" Nina asked.

"The what?"

Benjamin heard Zoey's fork clatter onto her plate.

"You know, the way the store owners try to get that quaint fishing village thing going. Ye Olde Fudge Shoppe, Ye Olde Taverne, Ye Olde Johnny on the Spot."

Benjamin smiled. Nina always said funny things in threes. It was her rule of comic tautology.

"I, uh, guess I never noticed that stuff," Lara said.

"I hear Lara's got a charming boyfriend," Zoey said in the moment of silence that followed.

Benjamin raised his eyebrows in the direction of his sister. Was she being mean on purpose? Zoey was naturally sweet—almost too sweet—but she could be cruel when she got defensive. Maybe Lara was giving her the evil eye from across the table.

"How nice," Mrs. Passmore said. "Does he work at the restaurant with you?"

Nina snorted loudly. When Benjamin and Nina had followed Lara and her boyfriend, Keith, the bar they wound up in *had* served food, and technically Keith had been working—Nina had observed Keith in the middle of a drug deal. Benjamin wondered how Lara would answer the question.

"Actually, we broke up," Lara said. She didn't sound particularly sad about the fact.

"Too bad. He made such a good impression—right on my face," Benjamin joked.

"Well, he's in jail now."

"Jail?" Mrs. Passmore said.

As a fellow teenager, Benjamin felt compelled to change the topic of conversation. His parents were cool, but even they didn't take too kindly to ex-boyfriends in the slammer. "So, how's your apartment?" Benjamin asked.

"I'm getting kicked out the first of the month."

So much for changing the subject. Benjamin heard Nina snort again. He tried to kick her in the shin, but his foot hit a leg of her chair instead.

"The first is Sunday!" Mr. Passmore exclaimed. With every passing minute, he was sounding more like a sitcom dad.

Good, Dad, Benjamin thought. *You know your calendar.*

"Where will you go?" Mrs. Passmore asked.

"Who knows?" Lara didn't sound any more concerned about her pending homelessness than she had about her boyfriend's being a convict.

"Uh, could I have the rolls, please?" Zoey asked.

"Have you looked at any apartments?" Mr. Passmore asked.

There was a pause, during which time Benjamin assumed Lara was shaking her head. "I saw a couple. Nobody'll rent to me."

"Why not?" Nina asked. Unlike Lara, she sounded fascinated by the idea of a nineteen-year-old getting thrown out onto the street.

"Keith pissed off my landlady. Now she won't give me a recommendation."

"Oh, my," Mr. Passmore said. He sounded horrified.

Benjamin decided to try the subject-change thing again. "So, how about them Red Sox? Think they'll finally make it to the Super Bowl?"

Zoey pushed away her plate and unbuttoned the top of her skirt. "I feel like I'm going to throw up."

And not just because of the food. Zoey's nerves felt as though they'd been put through a deli meat slicer. In the last half hour, the Passmores had learned that Lara's boyfriend's

66

being in jail and her losing her apartment were the *good* news.

In her deadpan voice, Lara had also informed the family that she was a high-school dropout, had been arrested for shoplifting, and had only forty-three dollars and sixty cents to her name.

Zoey was grateful that dinner was over. She just hoped Lara wouldn't inform them during dessert that she was pregnant with Charles Manson's child.

"Jeff, will you help me with the coffee?" Mrs. Passmore asked. She stood and collected half a dozen dishes in her arms, waitress-style.

When Mr. and Mrs. Passmore were gone, Zoey, Lara, Nina, and Benjamin sat in uncomfortable silence. Nina looked so miserable that Zoey almost laughed. Her lips were pressed together in a tight line, and she kept squinting, as if she were trying to read the fine print on a pact with the devil.

Zoey noticed Lara staring at Benjamin. A moment later he moved his head so that it appeared he was staring back. Lara bounced in her chair, obviously surprised.

"Are you really blind?" she asked.

Benjamin leaned back in his chair and assumed a sort of James Dean pose. "No, this is just an elaborate ruse I've set up to gain sympathy," he said dryly.

Lara glanced at Zoey as if she was expecting confirmation.

"He's kidding," Nina said.

"But how did he know I was looking at him?" She looked from Zoey to Nina, waiting for an answer.

"I'm blind, not deaf," Benjamin said. "You can ask me."

"Okay, how?"

"Just a lucky guess, to tell you the truth." Benjamin sounded proud.

"Excuse me," Nina said suddenly. She jumped from her chair and race-walked out of the dining room.

When she was just beyond the doorway, Nina motioned frantically to Zoey.

"I'll be right back," Zoey said.

She found Nina standing next to the front door, clutching her stomach. She already had her coat on.

"I have to go," Nina whispered.

"Nina, no! I need you here."

Nina leaned against the door. A drop of sweat trickled down her cheek. "Zoey, I don't just have to go. I have to *go*."

"You mean . . . ?"

"One too many servings of sweet potatoes, if you know what I'm saying."

No wonder Nina had looked so miserable. "Why don't you just go upstairs? You can use the bathroom next to my room."

She shook her head. "This stink isn't going to confine itself to your tiny bathroom. Everybody'll know."

"Nina, digestion is a natural part of life."

Nina opened the front door. "Zoey, you're my best friend, and I love you. But I am not, I repeat, *not,* going to have a diarrhea explosion under the same roof as my boyfriend."

Zoey's shoulders slumped. She couldn't blame Nina for leaving. There were some things she definitely wouldn't want to share with Lucas.

"Well, thanks for coming."

"Lucas will be here soon anyway, right?"

Zoey had forgotten that Lucas was coming. "Yeah. He should be here soon."

"Will you make up some excuse for Benjamin? Tell him I had to de-ice Claire or something."

Zoey grinned. "Sure thing. Feel better."

Nina saluted. "Good luck. I'll call you tomorrow."

"Are we going to the mall?" Zoey asked.

"Where else?" Nina jogged down the front path, apparently intent on making her way to a private bathroom as quickly as possible.

Zoey got back into the dining room at the same time as her parents. "Here we go. Coffee and pie," Mr. Passmore said from the doorway.

Mrs. Passmore handed around cups and saucers. Zoey took the coffeepot and walked around the table, pouring for each person.

When she sat back down, her dad cleared his throat for what seemed like nearly thirty seconds.

"Are you okay, Dad?" Benjamin asked. "Should we administer the Heimlich maneuver?"

"Let's have a little talk, kids," Mrs. Passmore interrupted. Her smile was so big and fake that it looked as if her face muscles were going to go into spasm.

"Darla and I had a brainstorm in the kitchen," Mr. Passmore said, wearing the same weird smile as Zoey's mom.

Zoey glanced back at her mother, who was now pouring spoonful after spoonful of sugar into her coffee.

Benjamin looked wary. "Don't keep us in suspense, Dad."

Zoey wasn't sure she wanted to know the content of this so-called brainstorm. The last time her parents had sat them down for a talk, they'd announced their separation.

"You know we have that big storage room over the garage," Mr. Passmore started. "Actually, you don't know that, Lara. But we do."

"Uh-huh," Lara responded. She topped off her cup with cream, making the coffee overflow into her saucer.

"We're not using the space for anything," Mrs. Passmore said. "There are just some old bikes and broken sleds in there."

"So, seeing as you're kind of down on your luck in terms of a place to live, we thought you might want to move in," Mr. Passmore concluded.

"Temporarily," Mrs. Passmore added quickly.

Zoey pinched herself to make sure she wasn't having a nightmare. She must have heard wrong. There was no way, no possible way, that her parents could have just suggested that Lara McAvoy should *move into their house*.

Lara looked dazed. "You mean me?"

"Everybody else already lives here," Benjamin pointed out with a wry smile.

"The room is heated. And you can share Benjamin's first-floor bathroom. Or Zoey's, upstairs."

Could this night get worse? Zoey wondered. She felt her fingernails digging into the palms of her hand. Lara wouldn't say yes, would she? A girl like that wouldn't want to live with a boring, humdrum family. No way. She'd probably rather shack up with some tattooed, spaced-out loser in a flophouse.

"Would I have to, like, pay you?" Lara asked. She sounded interested. Very interested.

"Oh, no," Mr. Passmore said.

"And it's just temporary," Mrs. Passmore repeated. "Until you find a place you like better."

"In the meantime, maybe you can study for your GED," Mr. Passmore suggested. "Zoey's a terrific tutor."

Great. Now they want me to be her personal tutor. Her parents must have roasted their brains along with the turkey.

"So, what do you say?" Mr. Passmore asked.

Lara smiled for the first time since she'd come into their house. "Sure. Why not?"

"A toast to family," Mr. Passmore said, lifting his coffee cup. Zoey mechanically raised her cup for the toast. *So much for just one night*, she thought grimly.

Six

Zoey was staring at the empty wall next to her dormer window. She used to write inspirational quotes on yellow Post-it notes and tack them up on her wall, but she'd taken them down when she'd caught her mom cheating on her dad. At the time, she'd thought that pondering the meaning of life was a worthless pursuit. Now she wished she had some helpful tidbit on her wall, something about life being absurd.

There was a knock on her door. "Zo, can I come in?" Lucas called softly.

She reached over from her bed and opened the door. "Sure."

Lucas sat down behind her. He pulled her back against his stomach, then wrapped his arms around her. She felt his chin resting lightly on her shoulder, and she reached up to touch his hair.

"I'm glad you're here," she said.

"Benjamin told me about Lara's moving in. Sounds like I missed quite a scene."

Zoey shrugged. "Nothing unusual. Just my parents being total idiots."

"Are you going to be okay with this?"

"I don't have much choice. They didn't exactly ask my opinion before they informed us of their brilliant idea."

"You're probably not going to want to hear this, but I kind of admire your dad for what he's doing," Lucas said.

Zoey pulled away. She moved to the edge of the bed and sat on her heels, facing her boyfriend. "You're right. I don't want to hear that."

Lucas ran his fingers through his blond hair, sighing. "See, Zoey, your dad has always been there for you."

"Yeah. But that doesn't mean I want to bunk up with his love child."

Lucas closed his eyes before he spoke. "Think about how *she* feels, Zoey. I mean, I *know* what it's like to have a dad who might as well be nonexistent." He opened his eyes. "It hurts."

Zoey rose and walked on her knees to Lucas's side of the bed. She took his head in her arms, cradling it against her chest. "I'm sorry, Lucas." He moved her arms around her waist, clutching little bunches of her wool sweater in his fists.

Lucas's father was a cold, inflexible man. He didn't believe in showing any tenderness toward his son, and he expected Mrs. Cabral to obey him without question. The only things Mr. Cabral seemed to care about were lobstering and the honor of his family. When everyone had believed Lucas had been driving the car the night Wade was killed, Mr. Cabral had planned to banish Lucas from his childhood home.

"And now Lara's got a chance," he continued.

"I know what you're saying. I really do. But I still don't want Lara to live with us. She can get to know my dad on her own time."

Lucas shook his head. "You're going to have to handle this in your own way, Zoey," he said quietly. "But if you want my advice, I'd suggest you try to imagine what it's like to be Lara McAvoy right about now."

Except for a few weary-looking housewives, the 10:25 A.M. ferry was almost empty. Aisha, Zoey, and Nina went into the boat's small closed-in area to shield themselves from the icy wind.

Aisha pulled off her hat and mittens. The air in the cabin was hot and stuffy, making her wish she hadn't worn such a thick sweater. The mall would probably be overheated, too.

"Don't you just love shopping the day after Thanksgiving?" she said.

"Almost as much as going to the gynecologist," Nina said.

"I'm serious," Aisha insisted. "It's like we're part of the big picture. We eat turkey, sleep, wake up, and go to the mall with the rest of America."

"Then we go home and see some really dumb thing on the local news about how everyone went to the mall today."

"Exactly," Aisha said. She was still feeling

warm and fuzzy from her Thanksgiving dinner with Christopher. Once he'd washed the lipstick off his face, everything had gone perfectly.

"Let me pose a question, Eesh," Nina said.

Aisha saw Zoey roll her eyes, but Nina didn't notice the gesture and continued. "According to the news, everyone goes shopping the day after Thanksgiving in order to get a jump on Christmas shopping. Right?"

"Right," Aisha said.

"Well, does anyone actually *buy* Christmas presents on this day? I mean, personally, I have never once bought a Christmas present the day after Thanksgiving."

"Yet every year, here you are, heading to the mall," Aisha said.

"Yep."

"Maybe you're just a natural procrastinator. I've bought *many* Christmas presents the day after Thanksgiving. Last year I bought my dad a wallet. The year before, I bought Kalif a Yankees cap. Today I plan to—"

"We get the point, Eesh," Zoey broke in. "You're perfect. Nina's a loser. We've known that for a long time."

Aisha raised her eyebrows at Nina. Zoey had been totally quiet since they'd met up, and now she was being mean. Very un-Zoey.

"Excuse her," Nina said, throwing an arm around Zoey. "She found out last night that the evil half sister is moving into her house."

"What?" Aisha yelled. Christopher had told

her that Lara was going to the Passmores' for Thanksgiving, but he hadn't said she was going to take up permanent residence.

Zoey nodded. "She's moving in. She's actually moving into my house."

"Temporarily," Nina said. "Benjamin told me it's only temporary. He said your mom stressed that point something like five times."

"She's sharing my bathroom." Zoey revealed the information as if she'd just told them she had leukemia.

"You'd better make some room in there," Nina joked. "The girl will need a whole cabinet just for her hair spray."

"What if she wants to borrow my clothes?" Zoey moaned.

"Somehow I doubt that situation will arise," Nina said.

Aisha's first reaction to this news was sympathy for Zoey. Her second reaction was to wonder whether or not Christopher would find Lara McAvoy attractive.

Zoey thumped the back of her head against the somewhat grimy wall. "My dad's lost his mind. Have I said that?"

"About six times," Nina reported.

"She'll probably turn tricks in her bedroom."

"Zoey, that's not fair," Aisha said.

Zoey didn't seem to care whether or not she was being fair. "What if her convict boyfriend shows up?"

"Convict boyfriend?" Aisha yelped.

"Remember Mr. Hair from Richard Felix's party?" Nina asked.

How could Aisha forget? The guy had been on his way to beating Benjamin to a pulp until Benjamin had managed a well-aimed kick to the groin. "Yeah."

"He's in jail. Lara announced it at the dinner table."

"Interesting twist."

Aisha could tell from Nina's vigorous nod that she was getting a kick out of the drama in Zoey's life. Then again, so was Aisha.

"What does Benjamin think of all this?" Aisha asked.

"He's being infuriatingly rational, as always." Zoey slouched in her seat, looking defeated.

"Maybe you'll actually like her," Aisha suggested. Someone had to be a voice of reason.

"I might like heroin, too. That doesn't mean I'm going to try it."

Nina pulled out a Lucky Strike. "Jeez, where's the Zoey we knew and loved? That sweet girl who believed in world peace, feeding the hungry, and loving thy neighbor?"

"Not to mention thy sister," Aisha added.

Zoey grabbed the unlit cigarette from Nina and sucked deeply. "She's back in the tenth grade, going out with Jake and thinking life could be summed up in a book of famous quotes."

*   *   *

78

Claire found her father at the dining room table. Friday's newspaper was spread out neatly in front of him, and he held a steaming cup of coffee in his hand. That morning he looked like the serious, workaholic father she was accustomed to. All signs of the giddy, infatuated teenager were camouflaged by his three-piece suit and silk Hermès tie.

Still, the mere fact that her father was sitting at the dining room table at eleven o'clock on a weekday morning was a clue that he'd undergone some major life change. Normally he was out of the house before Nina and Claire even came downstairs.

"Taking the morning off?" Claire asked.

Mr. Geiger smiled guiltily. "Sarah thinks I work too hard. She practically ordered me to sleep late and spend a couple of hours lazing around the house."

Perfect. Claire would seem rude beyond belief if she didn't take up her father's lead and talk about Sarah. And with the tiniest amount of strategy on her part, the conversation would flow exactly as she'd planned. Claire grinned as she ducked into the kitchen for a mug of coffee.

When she returned to the dining room, Mr. Geiger was staring into space.

"Sarah seems really great, Dad."

Mr. Geiger snapped to attention. "Isn't she wonderful? I feel twenty years old again."

Claire sat down and retrieved section C of the paper, which held the day's weather report.

"So why did you keep her a secret?"

"I just wanted to make sure that Sarah and I were going to be special to each other before I complicated things for you and Nina."

Special to each other? So much for that morning's nine-to-five businessman. Her dad was getting more corny by the day.

"Her son must be pretty bored out here," Claire said casually. She made a show of studying the barometric pressure for the previous day. "Not much happening weatherwise," she remarked.

Right on cue, Mr. Geiger frowned. "Why would Aaron be bored?"

Claire turned a page of the newspaper. "Come on, Dad. North Harbor isn't exactly New York City. There's not much for a seventeen-year-old guy to do here."

"Well, you and Nina and your friends seem to get along all right."

"Yeah. But that's because we've lived here forever. We all know each other."

Mr. Geiger set down his cup of coffee and frowned for a few seconds at an article about the rising cost of real estate in Camden. Claire could see the parental wheels turning in his head.

"Claire, I don't ask much of you," he said finally.

"True." Claire's heart rate sped up. This was the moment she'd been building up to.

"Could I ask a favor now?"

"Sure, Dad. What is it?" *As if I don't already know,* she added silently.

"Would you girls entertain Aaron while he's here?"

Claire took a sip of coffee, biding her time. "Jeez, Dad. I barely know the guy. . . ."

"You don't have to do it on your own," he said quickly. "You can get all of the island kids involved."

Claire grimaced. "How do you suggest I do that? I'm not exactly Miss Social Coordinator, in case you hadn't noticed."

"What are you doing tonight?" Mr. Geiger asked. He seemed to be holding his breath, waiting for her response.

"Well, I don't have anything planned. But still . . ."

"What about Nina?"

"She'll probably hang out at the Passmores', like she does every night."

"Why don't you have everybody over here?" Mr. Geiger suggested. He sounded so excited, Claire half expected to see a cartoon lightbulb form over his head. "I'm sure Aaron would fit right in with your friends."

"You mean, like a party?" she asked.

"Sure, why not?" Mr. Geiger had already removed his wallet from his jacket pocket. He took out three twenty-dollar bills and laid them on the table. "Buy whatever you need."

"I don't know. . . ."

"I'm going out with Sarah anyway, so you

kids can have the whole house to yourselves."

Claire sighed. "I'll have to talk to Nina. . . ."

"Please, Claire. Your old dad would really appreciate this."

She closed the newspaper and stood up, her mission accomplished. "Okay, Dad. I'll do it for you."

Mr. Geiger was staring into space again as Claire went back to the kitchen for another cup of coffee. She watched a lump of sugar dissolve in the hot liquid, feeling entirely at peace with herself. The impossible had happened. After weeks of boredom, Claire was looking forward to a Friday night.

Seven

At 3:20 P.M. Zoey, Aisha, and Nina exited the Weymouth Mall. Nina carried one small bag containing the new Smashing Pumpkins CD. Zoey carried one small bag containing a hard-cover book, *Why We Love to Hate Our Siblings*, by Dr. John Maxwell. Aisha carried many small bags, most of which contained Christmas presents for her family.

Just outside the mall, Nina sidestepped a baby stroller and narrowly missed getting mowed down by an old woman in an electric wheelchair. "Go ahead and beam us up, Scotty," she said. "There's no intelligent life down here."

"Ha, ha," Zoey answered. She was poised at the edge of the parking lot, scanning for the Passmores' van.

Aisha stopped next to Zoey and rested her bags on the sidewalk. "Uh-oh. We should have paid more attention to where we parked."

The huge mall parking lot was like a used car dealer's wet dream. "Man, every car in Weymouth must be here," she said. "It's like the familymobiles' equivalent of Mecca or something."

"Wait a second. Didn't we go into the mall through Dillard's?" Aisha asked.

"Yeah, we did," Zoey confirmed.

"Are you sure?" Nina asked. "Because I specifically remember buying cheese fries as soon as we got here. And the cheese fries place is, like, a mile away from Dillard's." Unfortunately, Nina felt as if she were still eating her jumbo order of fries. As it turned out, one should eat carefully the day after a sweet-potato debacle.

Aisha shook her head. "You're thinking of Katie's Franks. You got fries at Harry's, which is right across from Dillard's."

"Oh, right," Nina said. "You bought that rancid perfume at the cosmetics counter there."

"Tea Rose is not rancid, Nina. It's very organic."

"Just don't put it on in a confined space— such as Zoey's car," Nina requested.

"I'd love to stand here and talk over matters of olfactory concern with you girls," Zoey said, turning away from the parking lot. "But we've got a lot of crowded mall to cross before we're anywhere *near* the van."

Nina pulled open the mall door, steeling herself for the mass of people who always seemed to be moving in the opposite direction from where she wanted to go.

The next year, Nina promised herself, she would follow Claire's example and stay home with a book. Tradition was overrated.

*   *   *

By three-thirty in the afternoon, Jake McRoyan had jogged close to ten miles and done five hundred abdomen crunches. Now he completed ten last push-ups, finishing his set of one hundred. He flopped onto his stomach for thirty seconds, then did twenty more, just to see if he could. Since he'd stopped drinking, exercise had become a new, more alluring addiction. He wanted to be in his best shape ever in time for the state football championships.

Jake peeled off his sweatshirt, tossing it on the pile of clothes that approximated a laundry basket. As he stepped out of his track shorts, he realized that he almost regretted that it wasn't a regular school day. If it were, he'd have a whole two hours of football practice ahead of him.

Thanksgiving had been even more depressing than usual. No amount of turkey and mashed potatoes could change the fact that Wade's empty place at the table was a gaping wound in the family structure. And Jake's new knowledge that Mr. McRoyan regularly slept with other women made him resent his father's false cheeriness during the holiday season.

The previous year Jake had been able to escape to the Passmores' after sharing a strained meal with his mom and dad. But now that he and Zoey were history, he'd had to retreat to his room, where he'd watched *The Real World* on MTV.

The exercise had kept him busy for a few more hours, but he still had the rest of the evening to get through. Jake stepped into a hot shower, wishing he had someplace to go.

Jake positioned his head under the shower nozzle so that the hot water ran over his ears, blocking out any sounds from the outside world. He lifted the bottle of Agree shampoo and squeezed the liquid straight onto his short hair. With the excess lather, he soaped up his chest and legs.

Ten minutes later, he forced himself to shut off the water and get out of the shower. He wrapped a fresh towel around his waist, then wiped the steam from the bathroom mirror with the back of his forearm.

His cheeks were covered with two days' worth of stubble, but he couldn't think of a good reason to shave. The weekend was looking dead. For the last several weeks he'd been avoiding parties where there would probably be a keg, which pretty much ruled out going over to Weymouth and finding something to do. And he hadn't heard from anyone on the island since school had let out at noon on Wednesday.

He slipped into a clean pair of sweats and stretched out on his bed. He could do some homework, but that would bump him from the bored category and into the merely pathetic. Instead, he dug his TV remote control, which was starting to feel like a permanent appendage, out from under his mess of covers.

There was a beach party weekend on MTV, World Wrestling Federation on channel eight, a bicycle race on ESPN, and *Forrest Gump* on HBO for the twentieth time that month. He switched off the television. Maybe he could count the tiles on his ceiling. Or do some more push-ups.

"Jake? Are you out of the shower?" Mrs. McRoyan called from outside his door.

"Yeah," he called back.

She opened the door. "Claire called while you were in the shower."

"What did *she* want?" he asked.

Claire hadn't phoned Jake's house for several weeks. Not since the night of Richard Felix's party, when she'd coldly informed Jake that she'd cheated on him with Lucas. That had been the end of Jake and Claire. Looking back, Jake realized that he and Claire hadn't been much of a couple to begin with.

Jake had been looking for someone to fill the void that Zoey had left, and Claire had been . . . well, who knew what Claire had been doing. As it turned out, being lonely with someone else was even worse than being lonely by oneself.

"She and Nina are having a party tonight," Mrs. McRoyan said. "She said to come around eight."

Typical Claire. She didn't bother to ask if people wanted to come to her party; she simply told them what time to show up. He was surprised she hadn't given his mother a list of what he should bring.

Jake shook his head, laughing. If nothing else, Claire had given him a reason to shave.

Nina, Zoey, and Aisha had made the four o'clock ferry with exactly twenty-seven seconds to spare. Finding the Passmores' van had turned into an epic and ugly search that was followed by even uglier traffic on the way back to the parking garage. They'd all been quiet during the ferry ride to Chatham, which had been a relief after the pandemonium at the Weymouth Mall.

Nina dropped her down jacket on a chair in the front hall and headed for the kitchen. She'd been thinking about sweet-potato leftovers for the past twenty minutes—a minor miracle, considering her experience the night before.

Claire was standing in the kitchen, opening jars of salsa and pouring them into bowls. On the counter behind her were several bags of chips, a giant bag of miniature Snickers bars, a case of diet Coke, and a case of Coke.

"What's going on? It looks like a convenience store exploded in here."

Claire put the salsa in the refrigerator. "We're having a party."

"Could you say that again? It sounded like you said that we, as in you and I, are having a party." Nina pushed Claire away from the fridge and knelt in search of foil-covered sweet potatoes.

"You heard right," Claire said. "Call Zoey and Aisha, will you? I already told everybody else."

Nina turned away from the refrigerator. Her brain had started working again, in the process informing her stomach that leftovers were a bad idea.

"Claire, I think we need to rewind this conversation." Nina grabbed a diet Coke, then took her favorite Muppets glass from the cabinet above the sink.

"Which part didn't you understand?"

"You and parties go together like cats and water. Like Mark Fuhrman and Nelson Mandela. Like me and high-heeled shoes. What gives?"

Nina filled the glass with ice from the automatic dispenser in the refrigerator door, noting as she did so that Kermit the Frog's face was chipping.

"Dad gave me a sob story about how bored that Aaron guy is out here. He practically begged me to have everybody over tonight."

"Who cares if Aaron's bored? I'm bored all the time, and nobody gives it a second thought."

"You're just boring, period. There's no cure for that."

"My, my, Claire. You sound defensive. Is there something you're not telling me?"

Nina was sure Claire hadn't agreed to host a party because she felt sorry for Aaron Mendel. She obviously had an ulterior motive. Nina hoped that motive was *not* getting back together with Benjamin. Nina shrugged off the idea.

Claire had said that even *she* wouldn't go so low as to take her own sister's boyfriend.

"Listen, Dad asked me to have a party. I agreed. Blame it on the spirit of Thanksgiving, if you want."

Nina thought of Aaron's dark hair and hazel eyes. Even Claire had to have noticed the guy was gorgeous. She poured the soda, then stood waiting for the fizz to die down. "Are you after Aaron?"

"Am I 'after Aaron'?" Claire said in a disgusted voice. "God, Nina, you sound like a geek in an ABC after-school special." She ticked off reasons on her fingers. "First of all, Aaron is leaving town in two days. Second of all, he's the offspring of the Happy Homemaker, otherwise known as Dad's girlfriend."

"You haven't answered the question, Claire." Nina poured more of the diet Coke, then took a long drink.

"I'm doing Dad a favor, Nina." Claire opened the bag of Snickers and dumped them into a bowl. "If you want to waste your energy on paranoid delusions about my supposed scheming mind, that's your business."

Nina stared at Kermit the Frog. Claire had surprised her many times in the past. Just when Nina had convinced herself that her sister was the Wicked Witch of the West, Claire would turn around and do something really nice. Maybe this was one of those times.

Nina glanced at her sister, who was calmly

spreading crackers on a plate. Her face revealed nothing, as usual. Nina shrugged. The truth was that she didn't care whether or not Claire had a hidden agenda. Either way, Nina would get to make out with Benjamin in her bedroom. And since they'd be in Nina's bedroom, Nina would get to choose the music.

She was glad she'd had the foresight to buy the new Smashing Pumpkins CD. Maybe the annual day-after-Thanksgiving trek to the mall wasn't such a bad idea, after all.

Eight

According to Wallace Stevens (who sold insurance policies in Connecticut when he wasn't being a famous poet), there are thirteen ways of looking at a blackbird. There were also thirteen ways (or more) of looking at Claire and Nina Geiger's party. Here are eight of them:

1.

Jake was the last to arrive. He didn't want to risk getting stuck alone with Claire, so he'd decided to be fashionably late. Nina let him in, and he attempted to hang up his jacket in the already full front hall closet. Then he draped it over a chair instead. The first thing he noticed when he walked in the door was that a guy he'd never seen before was sitting next to Zoey.

"Hey, everyone, *Joke*'s here," Nina called out.

Jake flinched. Nina had been calling him *Joke* for the past three years, and it still annoyed him. "Hi, guys."

Claire stood up and went to a table of soda, ice, and glasses that she'd set up in the corner.

"That's Aaron Mendel," she said, pointing to the stranger.

"Nice to meet you," Jake said, shaking Aaron's hand.

"Likewise," Aaron replied.

"He's our dad's girlfriend's son," Nina explained.

"What do you want to drink?" Claire asked.

Jake took a Coke and sat down next to Aisha, who was on the floor next to the couch. The general conversation seemed to be centered around Aaron. He was explaining that he wanted to go to Harvard and thought he would probably major in philosophy. Jake stuffed a handful of cheddar-and-sour-cream Ruffles into his mouth. He couldn't imagine being the kind of guy who could get into Harvard.

As the discussion about colleges flowed around him, Aisha bent close to his ear. "Be nice to Zoey," she whispered.

"Why?" he whispered back. Jake was always nice to Zoey. Or almost always.

"You know how she and Benjamin have that half sister, Lara McAvoy?"

Jake nodded. He remembered Lara McAvoy as clearly as he remembered getting kicked in the groin during football practice. She'd been a big part of the most terrifying night of his life. In fact, she'd been a key player in his decision to stop drinking. Not that *she* was aware of that fact.

"Well, she's moving in with the Passmores. She's going to live over their garage."

Jake choked on his potato chips. "You're kidding."

"Nope. Zoey is *extremely* upset, although Benjamin seems to be taking the news in stride. As usual."

Jake nodded again. Lara McAvoy was going to be living on Chatham Island. He couldn't quite believe it was true.

2.

At first, Claire was congratulating herself on the brilliance of this strategic move. By the end of the night Aaron Mendel would be head over heels in love with her.

But halfway into the conversation about Harvard, Claire observed a disturbing phenomenon. She'd just explained that she herself hoped to go to MIT; Aaron had nodded politely, but he hadn't pressed her for more information.

Instead, he turned his attention back to Zoey. For the next ten minutes, Claire noticed that Aaron's gaze went consistently back to Zoey, sometimes even when someone else was talking.

Claire retreated to the kitchen, where she refilled the ice bucket and pondered this new development. Lucas and Zoey hadn't come together, because Zoey had gotten there early to hang out with Nina. When Aaron had arrived and they'd all gone downstairs, Zoey had immediately claimed a place on the sofa. Aaron had promptly plopped down right next to her.

At the time, Claire hadn't given Aaron's seating position a second thought. When *she* was in a place where she didn't know a lot of people, she also tended to sit on the couch. Couches were decidedly less conspicuous than chairs.

But now she realized that Aaron might not have been aware that Zoey and Lucas were, well, *Zoey and Lucas*. Unfortunately, there didn't seem to be a decent way to get that information across without looking obvious about it.

Claire tucked her formfitting turtleneck sweater more securely into her jeans. If she wanted Aaron Mendel to fall for her, the endeavor was going to require a little more effort than she had expected. Claire smiled. She loved a challenge.

3.

Benjamin sat in one of the Geigers' more comfortable armchairs. Nina, who was in the middle of a diatribe about Weymouth High's lunchroom, was on the floor in front of him, her back up against his knees. With one hand he lightly stroked the back of her head.

"And *that's* why I think eating in a school cafeteria should be banned nationwide," Nina said.

"Very practical, Nina," Claire said sarcastically.

Benjamin heard Nina inhale deeply, which he knew meant she was about to launch into her argument again. But Christopher spoke up before she got the chance.

"What do you say we play some poker, guys?" he asked.

"Strip?" Lucas asked.

"We are *not* playing strip poker," Zoey announced.

"For money," Christopher said.

Nina said no. Aisha said no. Zoey said no. After a moment, Claire said no. Jake agreed. So did Lucas. After another moment, Aaron agreed. For Benjamin, poker was not an option.

"Let's go up to my room," Nina whispered.

This arrangement worked out fine for Benjamin, who for once in his life felt almost glad that he was blind. He'd never liked poker, but he loved fooling around with Nina.

4.

Christopher surveyed the table. He knew that neither Jake nor Lucas was very good at poker. Aaron was the only possible threat. Christopher prayed that the guy had been too busy reading books by Kant and Hegel to learn how to play cards. Christopher was badly in need of some extra cash.

They played five-card draw at Lucas's request. Jake dealt. Christopher started the hand with two aces. He threw out three cards and was dealt another ace, as well as a seven and a four. He kept his face carefully devoid of any hint that he planned to clean up the table.

Unfortunately, nobody bet big. Christopher ended up winning a dollar fifty, which wasn't going to make him rich fast.

Lucas dealt next. Again Christopher threw away three cards. He ended up with a pair of threes and decided to bluff. This time everyone bet big.

Aaron won with three fives. Christopher lost four dollars.

Christopher was the next dealer. He got nothing. He drew only one card, hoping this tactic would make him a more effective bluffer. The card he drew matched nothing in his hand. Although he had squat, Christopher made his largest bet yet.

Lucas folded. Jake folded. Aaron raised Christopher's bet, then won with a pair of twos.

Christopher began to regret that he'd ever suggested a poker game.

5.

Aisha sat in the living room with Claire and Zoey. "How long are they going to play?" she moaned.

"Our company isn't good enough for you?" Claire asked dryly.

"It's not that," Aisha said. She opened a fresh can of original-style Pringles. "I can tell that Christopher is losing money that he *really* can't afford to lose."

"What're you, his wife?" Claire took the can of Pringles away.

"I'm with Eesh," Zoey said. "Playing poker is completely antisocial."

"Do you think I should attempt to break up the game?" Aisha asked.

Claire shrugged. "I couldn't care less."

"Definitely," Zoey said. "It's time for some group interaction."

Aisha grabbed the Pringles back from Claire. She took two and stuck them in her mouth as a makeshift duck bill. "Quack. Quack."

Claire sneered. "That's the kind of thing Nina would do."

"Thanks," Aisha answered with a sweet smile. She refused to be drawn into the war between Claire and Nina.

"Are you going to go in there and tell them to cut short the poker game, or what?" Claire asked.

Aisha ate the two Pringles, then stood up. "Jeez, Claire. I thought you said you couldn't care less."

6.

Nina nibbled on Benjamin's earlobe. She loved the little mewing noises he made whenever her teeth lightly grazed his skin. They were lying (fully clothed) on her bed. Benjamin had finally agreed to listen to Smashing Pumpkins on the condition that Nina keep the volume at a level that didn't threaten to burst his eardrums. She'd felt this was a fair compromise.

Benjamin turned his head, capturing her lips with his. For the next several minutes Nina concentrated on her own mewing noises.

"Now this is what I call a party," Benjamin said finally.

Nina smiled as she snuggled against Benjamin's chest. "Well, it's better than listening to people talk about Harvard or watching a dumb poker game, that's for sure."

Benjamin pinned Nina beneath him and kissed her neck.

"Okay, okay. So it's better than, like, anything else in the world," she admitted.

Claire's unwelcome voice brought Nina off cloud nine. "Nina! Benjamin! Everybody's leaving," she yelled.

Nina groaned. "Do we have to go down there?"

"Yeah," Benjamin answered. "But not before we do *this* one more time." He kissed her.

It was quite a while later when Nina and Benjamin went downstairs. By that time everyone else was gone

7.

Lucas wished they hadn't stopped playing poker. At least when he was losing money to Aaron, he hadn't had to watch the guy ogle his girlfriend in that cleverly subtle manner.

Finally it was time to go. Lucas couldn't wait to walk Zoey home. More specifically, he couldn't wait to walk her home and into her bedroom. He went into the kitchen to get the small amount of change that he had left over from the poker game.

"Can you believe that guy?" Christopher asked. "He plays cards like it's something he does every day."

Lucas shrugged. He wasn't in the mood to extol the virtues of Aaron Mendel. That is, if one considered playing good poker a virtue, which Lucas did. "See you tomorrow, Christopher."

"I'll be the one with the tin can, begging for change," Christopher said.

Zoey wasn't in the living room. Lucas walked toward the front hall with rising anticipation. He hadn't kissed Zoey since the night before. When he heard Aaron's low voice, followed by Zoey's laugh, he stopped. He couldn't believe the guy had the nerve to flirt with Zoey with Lucas just a room away.

"It was really great getting to know you tonight," Aaron said.

"You too," Zoey responded.

There was a pause.

"I don't have much planned for the weekend."

"Really?" Zoey's voice sounded slightly unnatural, as if she'd just sucked some helium.

"Yeah. And I was wondering if you'd like to go to a movie or something."

Lucas felt his anger rise from a simmer to an all-out boil. He stepped into the front hall, ready for a fistfight. "Excuse me, that's my *girlfriend* you're talking to," Lucas said loudly.

"Zoey's your girlfriend?" Aaron looked surprised. "I didn't know. You two didn't seem—"

"Well, now you know," Lucas spat. He moved menacingly toward Aaron. "So keep your hands *and* your eyes off her."

"Lucas!" Zoey shouted. She turned to Aaron. "Please pardon my boyfriend. He seems to be reliving some scene from the age of the Neanderthals."

Lucas gulped. Zoey looked very, very angry. Even furious, a less optimistic person might have said.

8.

Zoey heard Lucas running to catch up with her. She'd stormed out of the Geigers' without saying good-bye to anyone.

She absolutely couldn't believe the way Lucas had acted—as if he owned her. As if she weren't a living, breathing human being who could accept or decline an invitation to a movie on her own. Of course she would have declined. Wouldn't she?

"Zo, I'm sorry." Lucas was walking next to her now. He sounded slightly out of breath.

She didn't respond. They walked in silence for almost two blocks. When Lucas tried to put his arm around her, she moved sideways.

"Really, Zoey. I'm sorry. I guess I kind of overreacted."

Zoey stopped. "Is that what you call treating me like a possession and humiliating me in front of a virtual stranger? Overreacting?"

Lucas bit his lip. "Zo, it's just that he was staring at you *all night*. He was practically drooling."

"He was not, Lucas," Zoey said firmly.

She had noticed Aaron looking at her, though. A lot. And each time she'd caught him staring, a weird sort of tingle had worked its way lightly through her body.

"Can you forgive me? I'm so in love with you that I get crazy sometimes."

Zoey nodded. She let Lucas put his arms around her. "Let's just forget the whole thing ever happened," she said.

"Thanks, Zo. You're the best."

As Lucas kissed her under the stars in the cold Maine night, Zoey thought of Aaron's hazel eyes.

I would have said no to the date, she assured herself.

Zoey

Rites of passage? That's a big question. Maybe Dr. John Maxwell has written a book about the subject. <u>Why We Love to Hate Rites of Passage</u> has a nice ring to it.

Last year it would have been easy for me to name all the major rites of passage:

1. Getting my period
2. Losing my virginity
3. Going to college
4. Getting married
5. Having a baby

I've only gone through number one on that list, although Lucas pushes me toward number two every chance he gets.

But these days I'm realizing that rites of passage have more to do with what's going on inside than they do with external events. I think I first started to notice this when I fell out of love with Jake and in love with Lucas. That was like, wow, I'm the sort of person who will callously break someone's heart if I find myself irresistibly attracted to another person.

I wasn't happy to discover this fact about who I am, but at the same time, the whole thing was liberating. All of a sudden I was Zoey. I mean, for years I'd just gone through life doing everything exactly the way people expected me to. Then one day I turned into this person who makes people say, "What is she thinking?" And once you've turned that corner, going from being just someone to being totally and completely you, it's impossible to go back.

Dealing with the fact that my parents are lowly humans who make mistakes like the rest of us was another rite of passage I'm not likely to forget soon.

And now I've got to face the fact that my half sister is going to be a part of my life. This

development isn't really
a passage. It's more of a
long, dark tunnel with no
light at the end of it.

Nine

Zoey stopped at 729 Independence Street. She'd been in Weymouth for almost an hour, walking up and down every street in the neighborhood *except* Independence. The building had four stories and was built of red brick, with crumbling steps leading to a once-white front door. Nina had told her that Lara McAvoy lived on the fourth floor, in what Nina assumed was a very small apartment.

According to Dr. John Maxwell, author of *Why We Love to Hate Our Siblings*, it was important that Zoey try to get to know the sibling in question in said sibling's own environment. Zoey didn't have much hope for the experiment, but since she'd paid $19.95 for Dr. Maxwell's advice, she figured she'd at least make an effort. A small, short effort.

Over her shoulder Zoey carried an empty L.L. Bean duffel bag that she planned to loan to Lara for the move. She swung the bag nervously and heard some loose change clink at the bottom. She decided against unzipping the bag to see how much was there. If Lara had been telling the truth about her bank account, she needed every penny she could get her hands on, and who was Zoey to begrudge her a couple of pennies and dimes? Of course, Lara's financial burden would be considerably lightened by getting free room and board.

Zoey's heart pounded as she climbed the four flights of stairs. She couldn't imagine her dad going up these same stairs, in less than twenty-four hours, to bring Lara McAvoy and all of her worldly belongings into their lives.

At the door of Lara's apartment, Zoey froze. Did she really want to do this? *Remember what Dr. Maxwell says*, a voice she recognized as her conscience whispered. Zoey knocked.

After almost a minute with no answer, Zoey began to relax. Lara wasn't home. Zoey had tried to "form a bridge," as the doctor suggested, but she'd been thwarted by forces beyond her control. She had done everything in her power—

The door swung open, and Zoey was confronted with Lara's wide blue eyes, which were noticeably bloodshot. Still, in jeans and a ZZ Top T-shirt, Lara looked considerably younger than she had two nights before.

"Uh, hi. Remember me?" Zoey said.

"My brain's not so fried that I'm going to forget a sister I just met two days ago."

Zoey bit her tongue to keep from saying that she was actually a *half* sister. Dr. John Maxwell would certainly not approve of squabbling over such petty semantics.

"Yeah, well, I thought maybe you'd need an extra duffel bag. For packing." She held out the bag.

"I do. Uh, thanks." Lara took the bag and moved back a few steps. "You can come in if you want."

"Sure." Zoey stepped into the apartment, feeling as if she were crossing over into the Twilight Zone.

There was one room, which was large but almost empty of furniture. An unmade bed sat opposite a small kitchen. Even from where she was standing, Zoey could see that the sink was piled high with dirty dishes. A door, which Zoey assumed led to the bathroom, was off to one side.

"I wasn't expecting company," Lara said. She looked almost embarrassed as her eyes flickered from Zoey to the sink.

Zoey tried to smile, and she forced her eyes away from the cluttered kitchen. "Oh, you should see my room. This is nothing."

"I'll bet," Lara answered.

Zoey tried to appear at ease as she finished surveying the apartment. Unfortunately, her hands were shaking and her breathing was shallow. She was hardly a portrait of cool self-assurance.

"What are those?" Zoey pointed to a group of unframed paintings that were stacked in threes against the wall next to the kitchen.

"I'm an artist," Lara said in the same eerie

111

monotone she'd used all through Thanksgiving dinner.

"Really? You didn't mention it."

Lara shrugged as she walked toward the paintings. "What's to mention? If you're not in a gallery, nobody gives a crap."

Zoey wasn't sure how to respond. She wasn't even sure why she was still there. Her plan had been to drop off the bag and leave immediately.

"So, uh, how's the packing coming?" she asked. Lara hadn't asked her to sit down, not that there was really anywhere to sit, so she leaned against the wall, her arms folded in front of her chest.

"I haven't started. I'll just throw everything in a couple of boxes tomorrow morning."

Zoey nodded. Aside from a stereo and the paintings, it didn't look as though Lara owned much. Apparently Lara didn't have much of a nesting instinct.

Lara seemed to read Zoey's thoughts. "Keith stole a bunch of my stuff," she explained.

"Oh, that's too bad."

"Yeah. At least he didn't take any of my paintings. Or my stereo. He probably would have taken that if he'd thought he could get the thing down four flights of stairs without anybody calling the cops."

This was the most she'd heard Lara say at one time, but again Zoey had no idea how to respond.

She'd never been so unnerved by the

112

presence of another person, but somehow she couldn't make herself flee the apartment. She felt as if she were driving by the scene of a bad car accident. She knew she shouldn't look, but morbid fascination forced her to slow down and gawk.

"C-Could I, like, look at a few of your paintings?" Zoey stammered.

"You'll probably think they're pretty strange," Lara said, but she bent and picked one up. She moved to the two windows at the opposite side of the room and held the canvas in the light.

Zoey felt her eyes widen as she stared at the painting. Vivid shades of red covered the entire canvas, forming an abstract figure that looked sort of like a medieval demon. Lara's name was scrawled in black at the bottom.

"Wow," Zoey said after a few seconds. "That's really, uh, different."

Lara let out a sound that seemed halfway between a laugh and an expression of contempt. "I can do other stuff, too," she said. She went back to the stacks of paintings and extracted one. When she held it up to the light, Zoey was even more surprised than she'd been by the first. This painting was a landscape done in shades of purple and brown. The scene showed a lake just before dawn. Next to the lake, a girl sat naked and cross-legged.

"That's incredible!" Zoey said. She couldn't believe the same girl had produced both works. It made her wonder if Lara had a split personality.

"Yeah, well, this is the kind of stuff people

113

groove on. But the abstract works are where I'm really at." She dropped the painting as indifferently as if it were a pair of dirty socks.

Zoey glanced around the room again. This time she noticed streaks of grime on the windowsills, as well as a mousetrap in one corner. A mildewy-looking towel hung over the bathroom doorknob, and a layer of dust seemed to cover every surface.

Now that she'd ogled the scene of the accident, Zoey was desperate to keep moving. Fresh air seemed a million miles, rather than four stories, away. She looked at her watch.

"I'd better get going. The twelve fifty-five ferry leaves in a few minutes."

Lara shrugged and flopped onto the tangled sheets of her bed. "Whatever."

"Well, thanks for showing me the paintings."

Again Lara shrugged. "Thanks for the duffel. You'll get it back tomorrow."

Zoey edged toward the door. "Right. I guess I'll see you tomorrow, then."

"I guess so," Lara said. She wasn't looking at Zoey anymore. Her stare seemed focused on the sink full of dishes.

Zoey took a last look at her half sister and slipped out the door. She wasn't sure what she'd learned by visiting Lara McAvoy in her rundown apartment, but one thing was definite: Dr. John Maxwell had his work cut out for him.

LUCAS

Well, that first erection in math class is definitely a rite of passage. And getting your butt kicked in front of half the school in the cafeteria. And having sex. Unlike most rites of passage, that's one I'm actually looking forward to. But seeing as I need Zoey's cooperation, which so far hasn't been forthcoming, I'm going to have to wait on the sex thing. Which leads me to another rite of passage: cold showers after a date. And in the morning. And in the afternoon.

Nina

Rites of passage? I think the
brutal circumcision of thirteen-
year-old boys in Africa falls into
this category. And periods. My
theory is that menstruation was
invented by Tampax. Or Satan. Or
Advil. And doing It, of course. Oh,
yeah. Big rite of passage. A girl lies
in the backseat of her boyfriend's
parents' Volvo and lets Mr.
Wrinkles enter the Last Frontier.
The next day he tells his friends,
she tells her friends, and by night-
fall the relationship is over.

If you ask me, rites of passage

should be called rites of pain. That's what it's all about, right? Pain. I mean, no one ever gives you a million dollars and says, "Spend this in one day. It's a rite of passage."

I'll never be circumcised, and I've already suffered through the entrance into womanhood. So that leaves doing It. But I'm going to hold off on that for a while. A long while. Not that the thought of It with Benjamin doesn't appeal to me.

I forgot one: my mother dying. That was a rite of pain if ever there was one. I'm still going through it. I guess I always will be.

Benjamin

Obviously, losing my sight was a major rite of passage. It's taken me years to get used to being blind, and not a day passes when I don't wish I had my sight. If nothing else, I wish I could see what Nina looks like now. The ~~alst~~ last time I saw her, she was about eleven, with skinny arms, braces, and hair that was going through an awkward phase. I'm sure she's beautiful now—in a Nina sort of way. She probably doesn't have the cold, perfect beauty ~~fo~~ of her sister (who doubles as my ex-girlfriend), Claire. I like to think of Nina's beauty as a bit wild and unpredictable, just like she is.

Speaking of Nina, I've had another rite of passage on my mind a lot lately. . . .

Ten

Aisha shifted her backpack from one shoulder to the other as she waited for Zoey to answer the door. She'd randomly selected and checked out several books of poetry from Weymouth High's library on Wednesday morning, and they weighed a ton.

Aisha was not a poetry person. She appreciated logical subjects, such as math and science. She could even deal with history if it wasn't too revisionist. But poetry required a touchy-feely instinct, which Aisha lacked.

Nonetheless, she had to choose and analyze a poem for English class, and Aisha planned on doing the assignment well. Zoey, a person who had the touchy-feely instinct in abundance, had agreed to help.

Aisha was about to ring the bell again when Benjamin answered the door.

"Hey, Aisha," Benjamin said, aiming his sunglasses in the direction of her face.

"How'd you know it was me?" Sometimes Benjamin's ability to imitate a sighted person bordered on disturbing.

"I smelled you."

Aisha lifted her arm and took a quick sniff. "I just showered an hour ago! Don't tell me I've already got BO."

Benjamin laughed. "Zoey told me you bought Tea Rose at the mall yesterday. The stuff smells from, like, a mile away."

"So you don't like it, either." Aisha sighed. Benjamin wasn't the type of guy who went around insulting expensive perfume for no reason. She should have bought the Elizabeth Arden instead.

"Anyway, Zoey's not here."

"What? She said she'd help me pick out an ultrasappy poem today."

Benjamin shrugged. "Sorry."

"Well, where is she? Off with Lucas somewhere?"

Benjamin shrugged again. "She's not with him. He stopped by about twenty minutes ago, looking for her. I don't know where she is."

Aisha groaned. "I can't believe this. I could have spent the afternoon with Christopher if I'd known Zoey was going to blow me off. Now I'm stuck all alone."

"I know I'm not much of a booby prize, but you can hang out with me if you want."

Aisha stepped into the house and deposited her fifty-pound backpack on the hall table. "Why not? Maybe Zoey'll show up."

"Aisha, your enthusiasm is overwhelming. Am I blushing?"

"Sorry, Benjamin. I didn't mean it like that."

He laughed. "You want to make it up to me?"

"Benjamin Passmore asking for a favor? This is new."

Benjamin looked embarrassed. "Well, I've been wanting to check out the Internet for a while, but I really can't do it without the help of someone who can see."

Benjamin had worked incredibly hard to get to the point where he could get through his daily routine entirely on his own. He was even able to use his computer to type up all his schoolwork. But there were some activities that were impossible for him to manage.

"I'm happy to help," Aisha said, heading for his bedroom. "But why didn't you just ask Zoey or Nina to do it?"

In his own house, Benjamin moved quickly and gracefully. Now he opened his bedroom door for Aisha and gestured with a flourish for her to enter. "They both do too much for me already. You know what I mean?"

"Yeah, I see your point. You don't want your sister or your girlfriend taking over the role of mother."

"Exactly." Benjamin flicked on his computer. "Okay," he said, moving from his desk chair so that Aisha could sit down. "We're ready to roll."

Aisha was familiar with the Internet. She'd used Claire's America Online account a few times over the last few months and had done some Web surfing. She'd found a lot of chat forums, where the idea was that like-minded

123

people could get together via modem and "talk" about their interests. But in Aisha's experience, most online discussions got ruined by some idiot hacker with a perverted mind who invariably insisted on typing charming sentiments along the lines of "blow me."

"Where to?" Aisha asked.

Benjamin seemed to hesitate.

"Don't tell me you want to download sex pictures or something," she said.

"No . . ." Benjamin started to say something else, then bit his lip.

"What's going on?" Aisha asked. "Do you have some deep, dark Internet interest that you don't want to reveal to me?"

"Can you keep a secret?" Benjamin asked.

"Sure. As long as it doesn't involve you cheating on Nina or Lucas cheating on Zoey."

Benjamin gave her a half-smile. "No, no, it's nothing like that."

"Okay, then, spit it out." Aisha's hands were still poised over the keyboard.

Benjamin leaned back in his chair. He seemed to be considering his words carefully. "There's this Braille periodical that the school library gets every month."

"Uh-huh." Aisha rested her hands in her lap. Benjamin was taking his time with this secret, whatever it was.

"It talks a lot about blindness. You know, what causes it, how to adjust to it, what related diseases exist—"

"So? You know all that stuff, right?"

"Aisha, if you'll quit interrupting me, I'll *tell* you."

"Sorry."

"Anyway, last week the magazine was talking about some, ah, experiments that are being done in Boston."

"What kind of experiments?"

"They think they might have found a way to reverse blindness that's due to certain causes."

Aisha took a deep breath. What was Benjamin saying? "And that's what you want to check into?"

He nodded. "Yeah."

"Wow."

"Yeah. Wow."

"Do you know exactly where these experiments are being done?"

"Boston General Hospital. Think you can see if they've got an Internet site?"

"Sure." Aisha's fingers were shaking slightly as she called up Yahoo, an Internet search page. She typed in the name of the hospital as well as the word *blindness*.

"Do you see anything?" Benjamin asked. He was bent toward the screen, as if being close to it would help him know what it said.

"Hold on. I'm getting there." Aisha moved the cursor down a list of Internet sites until she got to one that looked right. She used the mouse to double-click on "Boston General Hospital Blindness Project."

A moment later she told him, "I found it."

Benjamin took a deep breath. "Will you read it to me?"

There were several paragraphs. Aisha started to read the information, slowly and deliberately. She got to the bottom of the screen, then scrolled down for more. As she continued to read, Benjamin remained completely silent.

Finally Aisha stopped. "That's it. Do you think you qualify to take part in the program?"

Benjamin still didn't say anything.

"Uh, there's a phone number," Aisha said. "Want me to write it down?"

"Yeah. Read it to me, and I'll memorize it," Benjamin said.

Aisha read the number twice, then Benjamin repeated it back to her. "Got it," he said.

"Ask for a Dr. Rita Kaufman," she added.

Benjamin nodded. "Will do."

"So, you think you qualify?" she asked again.

Benjamin swallowed loudly, pressing a hand to his forehead. "I think so."

Aisha reached forward and hugged him. "Benjamin, this is incredible."

"It's a long shot at best," he said.

"But still—"

"Promise you won't say anything. To anybody."

"Not even to Nina and Zoey?" Aisha asked. She thought that if she were Benjamin, she'd be yelling out this news from the rooftops.

"*Especially* not to Nina and Zoey. I don't

want to get everybody's hopes up. Not until I know more."

"But Benjamin—"

"You said you could keep a secret," Benjamin reminded her. "Now swear you'll keep quiet about this."

Aisha groaned. She had a strong feeling that she was going to regret what she was about to do. "Okay. I promise."

Benjamin let out a sigh of relief. "Thanks, Eesh. This means a lot to me."

"Well, if you really think this is the best way—"

"I know it is," Benjamin interrupted. "So, can I count on your help for the next stage of this? When I figure out what the next stage is?"

She smiled. "Benjamin, you've got yourself a date."

Zoey didn't feel like going home when she got off the ferry at Chatham Island. And she felt even less like going to the restaurant, where she'd inevitably have to discuss Lara's impending arrival with her mom and dad.

She briefly considered going to Lucas's. But she was still irritated with him about how possessive he'd been at Nina's. His behavior had bordered on cavemanlike, which had been particularly humiliating in front of a guy as sophisticated as Aaron.

She also thought about going over to Nina's. But Nina would give her the third degree about what had happened at Lara's, and Zoey didn't feel ready to talk about her bizarre encounter.

She finally headed up Dock Street, passing Passmores' without even glancing in the door. Within minutes, the street became empty of houses and stores. On Chatham Island, isolation was rarely less than a block away.

Up until a few months before, Zoey had walked this road almost daily. Jake's house was on Leeward Drive, a little way past Town Beach. But that day Zoey veered off the street before she got to Jake's intersection.

Town Beach wasn't a popular hangout spot, and now that fall had set in, the stretch of semi-sandy beach looked lonely. Several small boats had been pulled in from the water. They sat overturned on the shore, covered by large canvas tarps.

Although the temperature was much higher than it had been the past few days, the wind blowing in off the water made her shiver. Zoey approached the row of forlorn boats, planning to use the side of one of the larger craft to shield herself from the wind.

As she neared, a sudden movement in the sky caught her attention. Above her head, a huge red kite dipped sharply, then curved upward again.

From down the beach, Zoey heard a cry of triumph. "Fly, birdie! Fly!"

She turned slowly. He was about a hundred yards away, wearing a bright yellow jacket and faded Levi's. The hand controlling the kite was high above his head.

Zoey stood staring at him. Aaron hadn't seen her yet. He was turned away from her, jogging in the opposite direction.

Walk away, Zoey, she told herself. *Just walk away.* She started back toward Dock Street, then turned around again. This was ridiculous. Why shouldn't she say hello to him?

It wasn't her fault that Lucas had a suspicious mind. Unlike her boyfriend, she'd never done anything that would give him a reason not to trust her. Lucas was the one who'd fooled around with Claire. *She'd* never even thought about kissing another guy.

"Aaron!" she called. Her voice was almost lost in the wind.

He turned his head and seemed to recognize her. "Zoey!" he yelled. The kite took a dive, and Aaron surged forward, trying to keep it in the air.

His eyes were turned to the sky, and Zoey realized that he didn't see the piece of driftwood in front of him. "Watch out!" she shouted.

"What?" The word was barely out of Aaron's mouth before his foot caught on the wood. He sprawled face first into the sand, bringing the kite down with him.

Zoey ran forward. She couldn't help laughing when she got close. Aaron was covered with sand, and small pebbles fell from his hair as he shook his head.

"I was trying to tell you to watch out," she said between giggles.

"Thanks for the warning," he said dryly. "I guess I look pretty stupid."

She shrugged. "Hey, kite flying is a dangerous sport. Not everybody's up to the challenge."

He laughed. "You want to sit down?"

Zoey hesitated. Okay, so she *had* thought about kissing another guy. Aaron Mendel, to be exact. But thinking and doing were miles apart. There was no reason she couldn't hold a perfectly friendly conversation with a guy who happened to turn her knees to jelly.

"Let's go sit behind one of the boats." She brushed away strands of hair that the wind had blown into her eyes and mouth. "Less wind."

Aaron picked up the kite, and they walked in silence to one of the small boats. Once they were seated, Zoey searched her mind for something to say.

"Listen, I'm sorry if I made you uncomfortable last night," he said before she had come up with anything.

"Oh, no. You didn't," she said quickly. "I mean, maybe Lucas was a little uncomfortable, but that's just because . . ."

Aaron's hazel eyes seemed to burn a hole through her. "Because why?"

Because you're gorgeous. Because he saw the way I was staring at you. Because even though I'm in love with Lucas, I'm dying to kiss you right this very second.

"Oh, well, he's a little suspicious of people he doesn't know. Don't take it personally."

Aaron nodded. "If you were my girlfriend, I'd probably feel the same way."

Zoey felt herself blush at the thought of being his girlfriend and everything that would go along with it. "So, you're leaving tomorrow?"

"Tuesday, actually. My dad's been in Japan on business, and it turns out he has to stay an extra couple of days." Aaron's fingers made little ridges in the sand as he trailed his hand along his side.

"You must be bummed. Chatham's pretty quiet this time of year."

"No, I'm glad to be staying. The scenery out here is great inspiration."

Zoey looked out at the bleak, gray ocean. She rarely thought of her surroundings as scenery. She took the water and the rocks as much for granted as the flowered wallpaper in her bedroom. "Inspiration for what?"

"Songwriting," Aaron replied. "Blues, mostly."

"Do you, like, play the guitar or something?"

"Yep. Play the guitar, sing—the whole bit."

Zoey absorbed this new information. "I'd love to hear you sometime."

"I'm not sure Lucas would think that was such a great idea." Again Aaron's stare seemed to penetrate some hidden, previously unknown part of her inner landscape. "He might interpret an innocent jam session as something more."

"Lucas doesn't run my life," Zoey said.

"There's no reason a guy and a girl can't hang out and be friends."

"I totally agree with you. But not all guys realize there's more to life than sex." He stood up. "I should get going. My mom will think I drowned or something."

The word *sex* coming out of Aaron's mouth had made Zoey's stomach do an uncomfortable flip-flop. A small part of her brain realized that the flip-flop signaled danger. But the big, stupid part of her brain really wanted to listen to Aaron sing.

She looked up at him. "Better luck next time with the kite."

He grinned. "Thanks, Zoey." Aaron took a step away, then stopped. "You know, I never travel without my guitar. If you decide you really do want to hear me play, I'll be around the Grays' place all weekend."

Zoey watched him walk away. Her mouth felt dry and her heart was hammering in her chest. Guiltily she thought of Lucas, the love of her life. The small, rational part of her brain started shouting louder. Zoey listened.

The matter was decided. She would not listen to Aaron play the guitar. In all likelihood, she'd never set eyes on him again.

Eleven

Benjamin sat in front of his computer for a long time after Aisha had left. He ran his fingers over the monitor, seeing in his mind the words that Aisha had read.

It was when his left arm became numb and his heart started beating in fast, erratic thumps that he realized he was having a panic attack.

In his dreams, Benjamin could often see. He saw sunsets, rainbows, the vast expanse of ocean that surrounded Chatham Island. But it wasn't all scenes from a Hallmark calendar. He also saw Zoey eating a bowl of cornflakes, his mother waiting tables in the restaurant, his father's graying ponytail. Occasionally he even saw his own face.

Then he'd wake to blackness. Sometimes— not very often—he'd reach for the switch on the lamp that was next to his bed. And then he'd remember: His whole world was dark, the kind of dark that other people experienced only deep in caves or locked in a tiny closet in the back of a basement.

He'd spent years learning how to live in that darkness without bitterness. But it had taken time, and more energy than he'd even known he possessed.

When he was twelve years old and he'd first realized that he'd never see again, Benjamin had felt like one of those black holes in space. He was a nonperson, an anti-being. There would be no more touch football with Jake. No more browsing in bookstores. No more ogling the copies of *Playboy* his father kept hidden in the garage. Everything he'd once loved had been shut away, stored like old memories in a keepsake box.

But slowly Benjamin had reconstructed himself. Day by day, cell by cell, he'd built the person he was now. The person who fended off the pity of sighted people with practical jokes and sarcastic one-liners. The person who could move so gracefully across Chatham Island that a stranger would never guess he was blind. From that black hole, he'd created the Benjamin that his friends, his family, and even Nina knew and loved.

If he regained his sight, just who would Benjamin Passmore be?

On Saturday night Nina, Benjamin, Zoey, and Lucas sat on assorted couches and chairs in the Passmores' living room. Nina had tried to maneuver herself so that she was sitting on the sofa with Benjamin, but he'd taken an armchair instead.

At that point, Nina had started to get off the couch so that Lucas and Zoey could sit together.

But Zoey had plopped into the other chair before Nina was all the way off the couch. So Nina
and Lucas had ended up on the sofa together.
Nina wasn't happy with the arrangement, and
she doubted Lucas was thrilled, either, but there
were only so many mean looks she could cast in
Zoey's direction before she gave in to the infe-
rior seating arrangement.

Saturday Night Live was on TV, and David
Spade was telling a really bad joke. "This show
should be banned," Nina declared. "Doesn't the
FCC have rules against comedy shows coasting
on the glory days of the nineteen-seventies,
when John Belushi was still alive?"

"Let's see what's on Nick at Nite," Lucas suggested.

Nina reached for the remote control. "Good-
bye, pathetic losers," she said.

"Wait," Zoey said. "Isn't B. B. King the musi-
cal guest on *SNL* tonight?"

"Yeah. So?" Nina changed the channel. "Aha!
I Love Lucy. Now this is comedy."

"Nina, you've seen every episode of *Lucy*
like nine times. Let's check out B. B. King."

"Since when are you interested in watching an
aging blues singer perform on a low-quality sound
stage on an even lower-quality show?" Nina
asked. On the screen, Lucy was begging Ricky for
a chance to be in his show at the Tropicana.

"Zoey's right. Let's go back to *Saturday Night
Live*," Lucas suggested.

"You're just sticking up for her because she's

your girlfriend. Benjamin, what do you think?"

Benjamin turned to Nina. "Sorry, what?"

"Should we watch Lucy or David Spade?"

"Why should I care?" he snapped. "I can't see either one."

Nina switched the channel back to *Saturday Night Live*. Benjamin's out-of-character harshness had taken the fun out of Lucy. The couch/armchair dilemma she could regard as a thoughtless oversight on his part. But an actual rude comment was a totally different story.

Benjamin was obviously mad at her. Or even worse, bored with her company. Maybe he resented the fact that it was Saturday night and he had to sit in a living room and listen to Nina make cutting remarks about David Spade. Maybe he'd rather be hanging out alone in his room, listening to opera. Or *not* alone in his room, kissing some other, more exciting girl.

"Listen, guys, I'm beat," Benjamin said. "I'm gonna hit the sack."

Nina felt as though Benjamin had taken a small, very sharp Swiss Army knife and inserted it directly into her heart. She'd stopped breathing by the time he paused next to the couch.

"Well, good night," she squeaked.

He felt for her shoulder, then leaned down and kissed the top of her head. "'Night, Nina. I'll talk to you tomorrow."

When he was gone, Nina stared at B. B. King, who was singing a revamped version of

Robert Johnson's "Love in Vain." She wanted to force herself off the couch and go home, but she seemed to have developed a sudden case of paraplegia.

Zoey stood up as the last notes of the song faded out. "I hate to be a drag, but I'm going to go to bed, too," she announced. "I've got to fortify myself for tomorrow's encounter with Lara."

Before Nina or Lucas could respond, Zoey was halfway out of the living room. "You guys stay as long as you want," she said.

Without another word, Zoey was headed up the stairs. Seconds later, Nina heard her bedroom door close firmly behind her.

Lucas looked almost as bad as Nina felt. "Some nights just weren't meant to happen," he said.

Nina switched off the television. She hoped that was all it was—one very, very bad night.

Claire turned off the TV. *Saturday Night Live* had hit an all-time low that week. So had she, for that matter.

For the first time in her life, Claire Geiger had sat by the phone and waited for it to ring. When waiting hadn't worked, she'd stared. At ten o'clock she'd actually picked up the receiver to make sure there was a dial tone. Twenty-two minutes later, she'd gone so far as to punch in the first five digits of the number at the Grays' bed-and-breakfast. She had a new sympathy for the kind of girl who never got asked out on dates.

Claire felt idiotic as she unbuttoned the red silk blouse she'd put on at eight o'clock. Who wore a silk blouse, fresh from the dry cleaner, to watch TV on a Saturday night?

She stepped out of her jeans, going over exactly what she'd said to Aaron the night before. *Call me if you're bored tomorrow night. I'll probably be around.*

Maybe he'd thought she was just being polite. Like her message had been, *Hey, I really don't want to deal with you. But since you're my dad's girlfriend, I've got to say something that sounds halfway hospitable.*

No. Claire knew guys. Her message had been crystal clear. She'd practically invited him to come over and make out. She might as well have tied a bunch of balloons to the front porch and posted a banner that read Aaron Mendel— For a Good Time, Call Claire.

The truth was lurking somewhere in the pit of her stomach, where she'd shoved it during the party the night before. Aaron wanted Zoey. Sweet, nice Zoey, who was madly in love with Lucas. Sweet, nice Zoey, whom Jake had never really gotten over.

Claire was beautiful. She was smart. She could even be witty when she felt it was required. And Aaron was a kindred spirit. She'd known that as soon as he'd winked and said that corny prayer at Thanksgiving dinner. He was a person who recognized that getting through life meant having more than one face.

She knew from the way he'd charmed her father and dazzled his mother that he saw the whole prospect of living as one long chess game. Just the way Claire did.

Yet he wanted Zoey. Simple, transparent Zoey.

Why?

Zoey's Erotic Dream

The night was shrouded in fog, but Zoey moved purposefully through the streets, intent on her destination.

She stopped when she saw the bar's green neon sign. It blinked on and off, momentarily lighting up the night like a gigantic firefly.

Inside, the air was heavy and filled with smoke. Zoey ordered a Budweiser from the Irish bartender. (In real life Zoey has never been inside a bar, much less ordered a drink. But this is a dream.)

The bottle was wet and cold in her hand. She made her way to a group of tiny tables in front of a makeshift stage. In the corner, one empty table seemed to have her name written on it. Zoey sat down.

She took out a Lucky Strike. Magically, a hand holding a Zippo lighter appeared in front of her face. Zoey lit her cigarette, inhaling deeply. (In real life, Zoey would never smoke a cigarette, Lucky Strike or otherwise. But this is a dream.)

Aaron walked out from behind a sagging black curtain. He sat down on a stool in the middle of the stage and settled his beat-up guitar in his lap. A dim spotlight highlighted the dark stubble on his cheeks.

He strummed a few chords, getting the feel of the guitar. Then he looked out into the audience. His hazel eyes locked onto Zoey's.

There was a subtle change in his posture. His spine straightened, and he held his chin high. Zoey blew a smoke ring, watching.

"This is a little tune I wrote up in Maine," Aaron told the crowd. "Until tonight, I've never had a reason to sing it."

There was scattered applause, and Aaron smiled at Zoey. He began the first few bars of the song, his fingers flying over the strings of the guitar. Then he stopped and leaned toward the microphone.

"By the way, folks, this song is titled 'Zoey.'"

Sunday

10:00 A.M.

Mr. Passmore and Lara board the car ferry at Weymouth.

10:40 A.M.

Mr. Passmore and Lara arrive at the Passmores' house. Mr. Passmore carries two enormous Hefty bags, a large box, and Zoey's L.L. Bean duffel in from the car. Lara carries a mini faux-leather backpack.

10:42 A.M.

Lara receives a lukewarm welcome at the Passmores'.

11:00 A.M.

Nina drops by the Passmores', ostensibly to read to Benjamin. In fact, she wants to check out Lara.

11:15 A.M.

Aisha drops by the Passmores', ostensibly to return a book she borrowed from Zoey. In fact, she wants to check out Lara.

11:30 A.M.

Lucas drops by the Passmores', ostensibly to bring over some sticky buns his mother made. In fact, he wants to make out with Zoey.

12:30 P.M.

Jake sits in his room, trying to think of a legitimate reason to drop by the Passmores'. None comes to mind.

1:00 P.M.

Claire stands at the railing of her widow's walk. She figures all of Chatham Island has probably found a reason to drop by the Passmores' and check out Lara.

3:30 P.M.

Jake decides he doesn't care whether or not he has a good excuse to drop by the Passmores'. He'll do it anyway.

Twelve

At 4:03 P.M. Jake stood at the base of the steps that led to the room over the Passmores' garage, wondering how he'd managed to get from his house to the Passmores' without realizing what an incredibly stupid idea this was.

From what he'd seen, Lara McAvoy was bad news. Sure, she had a great body, and the kind of trailer-park good looks that get some guys hot. But she was not the kind of girl that Jake should be messing with.

It was 4:04 P.M. when Lara McAvoy appeared in the door of her new room and Jake realized that, stupid or not, he was about to talk to her again.

"Hey, bring that box up here, will you?" she called. She was wearing the tightest jeans he'd ever seen.

Jake looked over his shoulder to see if she was talking to someone else. She wasn't.

"Uh, this one?" he said, pointing to a box sitting next to the Passmores' van.

"Do you see any other?"

Jake picked up the box and started up the stairs. Whatever was inside thumped to one side.

"Be careful. That's my stereo," she ordered.

At the door of her room, Jake held out the box for her to take. But she stepped farther into the room and pointed to a small table next to her bed. "Just put it there."

Jake obeyed. "Uh, hi again."

"Hi." Lara sat down on the bare mattress and patted the place next to her. "You're Jake, right?"

Jake felt it was important to avoid the mattress. He walked to the small window at the far side of the room instead. "Yep. You and I hung out on Halloween."

Lara abandoned the bed. She picked up a bag of clothes and dumped them in the middle of the floor. "I remember. You ran out of my apartment screaming like a banshee."

Jake reddened. "Sorry about that."

Lara picked up a short black leather miniskirt and carried it to the closet. As he watched her put the skirt on a hanger, Jake had a vivid image of the way Lara's thigh had looked the night he'd been in her apartment. She'd been wearing something similar.

"So what brings you here, Jake?" she asked.

Jake shrugged. "I don't know."

Lara raised an eyebrow. "Have a seat on the bed. I promise I won't bite."

Jake moved to the bed, and Lara sat beside him. Close beside him. "It's weird being over here. I haven't been in this house for a long time," he said.

"We're in the garage."

146

"Well, I haven't been in the house *or* the garage for a long time." He didn't know why he was sharing this information, except that no other coherent thought had formed in his brain.

"Why's that?" Lara asked.

"Zoey and I, we used to be a couple. For a long time."

Lara moved on the bed, which made her jeans stretch even more tightly over her legs. "Yeah?"

"It's ancient history now."

"Too bad." Lara leaned past him in order to reach a barrette next to the stereo box. When her breast brushed his cheek, he inhaled sharply.

Jake swallowed hard several times. "Anyway, I wanted to thank you."

"Me? What for?" Lara held both of her arms over her head as she fastened the barrette in her hair. Jake stared at her breasts.

"That night we spent together—it changed my life."

Lara leaned back against her pillows, looking puzzled. "Am I forgetting something? Did we do it?"

"No, uh, no."

"Phew. I would've had to have been really zoned out not to remember sleeping with a guy like you." She stretched out her legs so that the tips of her toes were pressed lightly against his thigh. Jake stared at the red polish on her toenails.

"Uh, a guy like me?"

"Yeah. Big, gorgeous, hard-bodied." Her eyes moved up and down him as she spoke.

"Oh, ah, thanks. I think."

Lara wiggled her toes against his leg, which made electric tingles travel to another part of his body. "So, what's the big change?"

Jake moved his thigh so that there was an inch between it and Lara's foot. "After you contacted my older brother, Wade, I saw him."

"You *saw* him?" Her Zoey-like blue eyes were wide and incredulous.

"Yeah. In the graveyard. It was wild."

"You're kidding me." She was sitting up straight now.

"No, really. I saw my brother."

"But I didn't actually contact your brother."

"What do you mean? I was there."

"Jake, that ouija board stuff is total crap."

"But the letters! They spelled *W-a-d-e*."

Lara laughed. "That was me. *I* spelled *W-a-d-e*."

"How did you know?"

"Come on, Jake. Wade was one of the best football players in Maine. Everybody knows about his death."

"Oh." Jake covered his face with his hands. He felt like a total idiot.

"Don't feel too bad." She reached out and raked her fingernails through his short hair. "I can be a pretty convincing actress."

Jake nodded silently. "Well, I'm grateful to you, anyway," he said finally. "For that night, I mean."

"Why?" Lara looked suspicious. "I was a real jerk to you."

Jake hung his head. "Even if it was fake, that ouija thing made me believe that I saw Wade's ghost. Since then, I haven't had a drop of alcohol."

"Is that supposed to be a good thing?"

"I had sort of, uh, a problem with drinking for a while. And other stuff."

"A straight boy like you? I don't believe it."

Jake thought back to the night he'd done a line of cocaine. It had been the worst decision of his life. "Believe it. But that's all in the past."

Lara stroked his cheek with her hand, then ran the tip of her index finger across his lower lip. "Is it really?"

After dinner Lara went straight to 'her room over the garage. Mr. Passmore went to the restaurant so that Mrs. Passmore could come home. Zoey conferred briefly with Benjamin, and they both decided that their strained welcome dinner had been enough effort in Lara's direction for one day. Then they both went to their respective bedrooms.

Five minutes later the phone rang. Zoey raced downstairs to answer it, but Benjamin had beaten her to it.

"Lover boy," he said, holding out the phone.

For some reason that Zoey didn't care to identify, she was disappointed when the lover boy turned out to be Lucas.

"Hey," she said.

149

"How's it going over there? Is everything okay with Lara?"

"Aside from the fact that she can't hold a conversation and she asked if my dad minded if she painted the walls of her room black, yes, everything's fine."

Lucas laughed the sexy laugh that usually made Zoey want to go out the back door and climb the short hill to his house. "How about some company? It's lonely over here."

Zoey paused. It was Sunday. Aaron wasn't leaving until Tuesday. She could spend that night with Lucas and remind herself how much she loved him. Then the next day, when all her stupid fantasies about Aaron had been squashed by Lucas's kisses, she could go over to the Grays' and get Aaron to play her a song. That was all she wanted from him. A song.

"Keep the door open," Zoey said. "I'll be right there."

Thirteen

Monday morning was brutal. Zoey woke up at 4:43 A.M. and thought about Aaron for an hour. For the next hour she wondered whether or not Lara would leave a lot of hair in the tub when she took a shower. Zoey hoped not.

Benjamin had a dream that he could see. When he woke up, he promised himself that he would call Boston General that afternoon. Or Tuesday at the latest.

Lucas woke up needing a cold shower. Again.

Jake also woke up needing a cold shower. Getting dressed, he decided that Lara *was* the kind of girl he should be messing with.

Claire woke up earlier than usual but feeling refreshed. She decided she was glad Aaron would be leaving soon. He wasn't good enough for her, anyway.

Aisha got out of bed at 7:25. She dressed with her eyes half closed, which caused her to put on one blue sock and one brown sock.

Nina didn't remember waking up. But somehow she got herself to the ferry anyway.

*   *   *

Aisha, Zoey, and Nina sat huddled together on the *Island Breeze,* which was more commonly referred to as the *Minnow,* after the boat on *Gilligan's Island.*

There was an unspoken rule among the island kids that ferry time was up for grabs. Some mornings couples sat together. Other days it was guys and girls. There were also times when everyone was in a horrible mood, so they all sat alone.

That day Nina was in a good mood. Her worries about Benjamin had been assuaged by the hourlong kissing session that had taken place after she'd come over to check out Lara on Sunday. And then Benjamin had called before he went to bed, just to say good night.

Nina saw Claire standing at the ferry's railing. No doubt she was either contemplating the weather or thinking up new ways to terrorize orphans.

"Do you think they do it?" Nina asked Aisha and Zoey.

"Who?" Aisha looked up from her math homework, which was flapping precariously in the breeze.

"My dad and Sarah. Who else do we know who might be doing it?"

"You mean, are they having sex?" Zoey said.

"No, dancing the polka. Of course having sex."

"Definitely." Aisha erased a number in her equation.

"Probably, but not definitely," Zoey said.

"Why not definitely?" Nina asked.

Aisha's paper flew off her lap. She groaned and scurried after it. Nina noticed that she was wearing one blue sock and one brown sock.

"Maybe they want to wait till they're married," Zoey suggested.

"Married! Watch your language." Nina gagged.

"I thought you *wanted* your father to get remarried." Zoey shut *The Scarlet Letter*, which had been open in her lap.

"I do. But to a woman, not a midget."

"Sarah is *not* a midget."

Aisha had returned. Her math homework was now covered with muddy water from the puddle in which it had fallen. "Even if she were, she'd still be a woman."

"Just think, Aaron would be your stepbrother," Zoey said in a voice that a romance novel would have described as *dreamy*.

"I don't think I want a stepbrother. Having a sister is punishment enough."

"I bet he knows lots of cute guys," Zoey said. She returned her book to her backpack.

"So what?"

"So it never hurts to know cute guys."

"What are you talking about? I've got Benjamin. You've got Lucas. Eesh has Christopher. Plus there's Joke. We've got plenty of cute guys around."

Zoey shrugged. "You can never be too rich, too thin, or have too many cute guys around."

"I object to that statement," Aisha said.

"At least, I object to the too thin part."

"Yeah. Have you seen Kate Moss lately?" Nina demanded. "She's like a stick figure with hair."

"A stick figure with hair who's going out with Johnny Depp," Zoey pointed out.

Aisha shook her head. "They broke up. I read it in *People* magazine."

Nina was still stuck on the image of her fifty-year-old, slightly pot-bellied dad naked. Not a pretty picture. "The thought of my dad doing it makes me sick. Besides, when you're that age, body parts start to sag big-time."

"So they do it with the lights off," Aisha said in a matter-of-fact tone.

Nina regretted ever having started this conversation. "You know, Eesh, you're wearing two different colors of socks. Even Benjamin can do better than that."

For the last minutes of the ferry ride, discussion turned to whether or not Aisha should try to buy matching socks at lunchtime. The general consensus was that such a drastic measure was not necessary. In the end, Aisha had to go around school all day explaining that she'd slept late.

Monday afternoon Christopher paced from one side to the other of his studio apartment. His room was in the cheapest boarding house on Chatham Island; although it was small, he liked the fact that it was at the top of a miniature tower. The room had large windows on all sides, which gave him a great view of North Harbor.

At this hour on most days, Christopher would be hard at work. But his job in the athletic department at Weymouth High had ended when the weather had become too cold for the students to have gym class outside. He was out one job, which meant he was out one source of income.

Christopher picked up his checkbook. Usually he enjoyed skimming over the rectangular white pages where he faithfully recorded his deposits and withdrawals. He liked to see his stash of money for college slowly building, week by week, month by month.

But lately the number of deposits had been dwindling. Aside from the loss of his regular paycheck from the high school, Mrs. Gray hadn't needed much yard work done lately. The cash simply wasn't flowing.

Christopher groaned as he realized that there wasn't enough money in his checking account to cover December's rent. He'd have to dip into his savings account in order to keep a roof over his head.

It was time to come up with a new, even stricter budget. And he had to find another part-time job. Fast.

Zoey was acting weird. Really weird. Nina watched as Zoey dumped out her sock drawer to rearrange it for the third time. She had already cleaned her desk, alphabetized her bookshelf, and changed the sheets on her bed.

"So how's sharing a bathroom with Lara?"

Zoey folded a pair of green-and-brown argyle socks, which Nina privately thought belonged in the trash can. "Fine."

Not exactly the response she'd been expecting. "Did you figure out why she has the gallon bottle of peroxide under the sink?"

Zoey shrugged. She arranged a row of white tennis socks in the same place where they'd been before. "Who knows?"

"My guess is she uses the stuff to dye *all* of her hair to match the Cheap Blond number seven she's got on her head."

Zoey made a row of black socks. "Maybe."

"Or maybe she's got some really bad infections. *Unspeakable* infections."

Zoey didn't respond. She'd turned away from the drawer and was gazing out the window.

Nina tried again. "I saw Lara pouring kerosene all over the floor of the garage. And she was about to light a match. Should we be worried?"

Zoey looked at her. "Sorry, what?"

Nina swung her legs over the side of the bed. "You're hopeless, Zo. I'm going to go see what Benjamin's doing."

Zoey had started in on her jewelry box by the time Nina closed the door behind her. Nina hoped Benjamin could shed some light on his sister's spacey state.

Nina stopped outside Benjamin's door. She always liked to determine what music he was listening to before she went in, so that she'd have a sufficiently insulting remark at the ready.

But Benjamin's stereo didn't seem to be on, although Nina was sure she heard noise from the room. She frowned when she recognized Aisha's mellow voice, followed by a laugh from Benjamin. She hadn't realized Aisha was even in the house.

Nina lifted her hand to knock on the door, then stopped herself when she heard Aisha's voice again. *Maybe they're talking about me,* she thought. *Maybe Benjamin's going on about how he's totally in love with me.*

She pressed her ear against the door. Once more Aisha's voice came through loud and clear. "I wish I could kiss you right now," she said.

Nina stood completely still. She hadn't heard what she'd thought she'd heard. She simply had not. Obviously she was losing her hearing. Or else she was schizophrenic. She'd read somewhere that schizophrenia usually set in during the teen years.

"You're turning me on," Aisha said.

Benjamin laughed and murmured something that Nina couldn't make out.

Moments later she heard Aisha again. "Watch what you say. Other people might be listening."

"This is great," Benjamin responded.

"Want to get together somewhere more private?" Again Aisha's voice. "Name the time. I'll be waiting."

Nina felt bile rise in her throat. She wasn't losing her mind. Aisha and Benjamin were alone in Benjamin's room, and they were flirting.

Flirting. No, that was a euphemism for what they were doing. That was like referring to menstruation as "the monthly visitor." Or saying that Saddam Hussein "had a temper." Or remarking that Hugh Grant had "met" Divine Brown on Sunset Boulevard.

Aisha and Benjamin were fooling around. They were making out. They were . . .

Nina didn't want to contemplate the extent of what they might be doing.

She ran from the house at top speed and didn't slow down until she was in her bed, under her covers, with Nine Inch Nails playing at top volume to cover the sound of her sobs.

Zoey's room was clean. Her laundry was washed, dried, and folded. She'd plucked her eyebrows, painted her toenails, and given herself a pure mineral clay facial. The digital clock by her bed showed 8:00 P.M.

If she was going to go see Aaron, it was now or never. If she stayed at home, she could give herself a French manicure, or trim her bangs, or try out her mom's leg waxing kit. Or she could go to the Grays', where Aaron was probably already packing his bags.

She rummaged in her desk drawer for a nail file, pondering the wisdom (or lack thereof) of going to see Aaron. On the one hand, his feelings might be hurt if *nobody* bothered to say good-bye. Zoey hated it when people had their feelings hurt. Plus she really wanted to hear him play the guitar. How often did she get the chance to meet a real live blues singer?

On the other hand, the previous night she'd had another dream about Aaron. She'd woken up feeling sweaty and disoriented, and not thinking about Lucas at all.

But dreams didn't mean anything. They were unconscious thoughts that had absolutely nothing to do with everyday life. And in everyday life, Zoey was a faithful, devoted girlfriend. She shouldn't *not* do something just because she'd had an inconsequential unconscious thought. And when she got home, she'd call Lucas. She'd make sure that *he* would be the star of her dreams that night.

Mr. Gray answered the door. "Hi there, Zoey. Aisha's in her room."

Zoey silently thanked Mr. Gray for not being the kind of dad who felt compelled to ask his daughter's friend a million questions about school, family, blah, blah, blah. He usually cut to the chase, then went back to whatever he'd been doing.

Zoey walked down the hall toward Aisha's bedroom, which was near the back of the house. But as soon as she heard Mr. Gray's footsteps receding, she retraced her path and ran silently up the front staircase.

She paused at the second floor. Until this moment, she hadn't considered that she didn't know which of the guest rooms Aaron was staying in. She looked from left to right, undecided about how to proceed. Then she heard the sound of a guitar coming from a room at the west side of the house.

Zoey tiptoed down the hall, following the music. By the time she stopped in front of Aaron's door, Zoey was so nervous that she could barely breathe.

She pasted a fake, cheery smile on her face and knocked on the door. As soon as she saw Aaron, Zoey knew that this so-called friendly visit had not been a good idea. But she couldn't turn around and run, so she tried to be as casual as possible.

"Zoey!" He sounded surprised.

"Hi, I thought I'd come say good-bye. You still owe me a song." The words came out in a rush, but at least they got out.

He motioned her inside, a big grin on his face. "I'm glad you did." He paused. "Lucas is okay with this?"

Zoey coughed. "Oh, yeah. He, ah, wanted to come himself," she lied. "But he's got a test tomorrow. A math test. And he's terrible at math."

When Aaron laughed, Zoey observed that his hazel eyes seemed to light up the entire room. *Trite but true,* she thought.

"I get the picture," he said.

"But he, ah, sends his regards. He said to have a safe trip and everything."

"Great." Aaron nodded. "Well, have a seat. Please."

Zoey perched at the edge of his big double bed. Aaron sat down next to her, leaving at least two feet between them. He set the guitar in his lap. Zoey saw that his feet were bare. She felt a bizarre urge to study the small tuft of hair on his big toe.

"So, am I going to get to hear you play?"

"Absolutely. I love a captive audience."

Zoey began to relax. So far their exchange couldn't have been more innocent. Aaron even wished she'd brought Lucas with her. Obviously he wasn't any more interested in her than she was in him.

Aaron played a few chords. "I was playing something earlier that made me think of you, actually," he said.

Zoey gulped. Aaron had been thinking of her, maybe at the exact moment that she'd been thinking of him. But people thought about other people every day. Thinking was a natural, healthy part of life. "Really?" she said, trying to sound indifferent.

"Yep. Bessie Smith's 'Lady Luck Blues.'" He kept strumming the guitar strings, as if he hadn't decided what he wanted to sing yet. "She's the queen of the blues, you know."

Zoey didn't know. But she wasn't about to

admit it. "Will you sing it?" she said instead.

He grinned. "Sure, but the words sound kind of funny coming from a guy. Just close your eyes and put yourself in the song."

Zoey followed his instructions. When he started to sing, her heart skipped at least two beats. His voice was low and husky, just like his laugh. She tried to follow the words, but every one of her senses was focused on the sound of his voice.

When his voice trailed off at the end of the song, Zoey opened her eyes. The only words of the song that stuck in her mind were *lady luck, man, trouble,* and *girl.*

"That was incredible," she whispered.

Aaron set down the guitar. "Thanks. But I've got a long way to go before I'm any good."

"Your girlfriends must love to listen to you sing," Zoey said. She hoped that hearing him talk about other girls would drill into her brain the indisputable fact that Aaron was nothing more to her than Nina's dad's girlfriend's son. A tenuous connection at best.

"Oh, well, no . . ." He seemed suddenly embarrassed, and a blush rose in his cheeks.

"What?" Zoey asked.

"It's kind of embarrassing."

"You can tell me."

"Well, I've never really had a serious girlfriend. I've never had a girlfriend, period."

Zoey felt as though she'd just been given an electroshock treatment. This gorgeous, intelligent, talented, *perfect* guy had never had a girl-friend. "Why?"

"This part is even more embarrassing. . . ." He picked up the guitar again and began tuning.

"It can't be that bad," Zoey said. She was still absorbing his admission.

"Well, uh, I don't really believe in sex before marriage. And these days that's not exactly considered a desirable quality in a boyfriend."

If Zoey had felt shocked before, she now felt as if she'd been run over by a steamroller. She didn't try to stop herself from placing her hand gently on Aaron's shoulder. "I can relate, Aaron."

He squeezed her hand. "Can you really?"

She nodded. "Yeah. It's something Lucas and I fight about all the time. He just doesn't understand that I'm not ready."

Aaron gazed into her eyes. "I wish . . . I wish I'd met you somewhere else, Zoey. You're the kind of girl I've been waiting all my life to meet."

Zoey found herself closing the space between them. She would kiss him once. Just one quick kiss. A kiss of sympathy and understanding between two people who were on the same wavelength. Aaron was leaving in the morning, and nothing bad could happen as a result of one tiny kiss.

She brushed her lips against his, then felt the answering pressure of his mouth. A shiver raced down her spine. But almost before it had begun, the kiss was over. Zoey felt dazed.

Aaron took her hand and lifted it to his mouth. He touched her palm lightly with his lips, then smiled. "Thank you, Zoey. I'll never forget that."

She knew it was time to leave, but she couldn't seem to make her legs work. "Well, have a good trip tomorrow. And have fun skiing." Not the most profound way to conclude the evening, but it was all she could think of to say.

Aaron raised his eyebrows. "Oh, I guess I forgot to tell you. I'm not leaving tomorrow. My dad has to stay in Japan, so I'm going to spend the rest of the holidays here with my mom."

A dull throbbing began in Zoey's head. "You're, uh, staying? Here?"

"Yeah."

When Zoey stood up, her legs were shaking. "We can't let that happen again, Aaron."

He stood beside her and lightly traced the line of her cheek with his finger. "I know, Zoey. That's what makes it so beautiful."

The List (Part Two)

Lucas	Aaron
I'm in love with him.	I _might_ be in love with him.
He's in love with me.	He _might_ be in love with me.
Hormones in overdrive.	Doesn't believe in sex before marriage.
Says he'll never cheat on me again.	Has never cheated on me.
Makes me feel all warm and liquidy inside.	_Might_ make me feel all warm and liquidy inside.

Fourteen

Benjamin didn't go to the cafeteria at lunchtime on Tuesday. Instead he made his way to Weymouth High's administration office. He'd memorized the entire layout of the school, so he traveled easily through the crowded halls. As he walked, he counted steps in his head. *Seventy-two steps from the men's room to the end of the corridor. Turn left. Fifty-four more paces to the second-floor office.*

Benjamin opened the door, aiming his sunglasses in the direction of the school secretary's desk.

"Good afternoon, Benjamin," the secretary said.

"Afternoon, Sandra."

Benjamin adjusted his sightless gaze. Sandra's voice had come from another part of the room. "I'm filing," she explained.

Over the last couple of years, Benjamin had developed a bantering rapport with the secretary. Since he'd missed almost two years of school, first because of his illness and then because he had been learning to cope with blindness, and then had worked his butt off to gain back lost academic credit, Benjamin's school records were extremely complicated. Sandra was the person who had to keep track of the mountain of paperwork that constituted Benjamin's transcript.

"How about a favor for a poor, helpless blind boy, Sandra?" he asked.

The secretary laughed. "You, helpless? Give me a break, Benjamin."

"Okay, so I'm not entirely worthy of your pity. How about a favor anyway?"

"As long as it doesn't involve illegally altering your school record, I'll see what I can do."

He heard Sandra close the file drawer and move to the desk. "I need to make a phone call. In private," he said.

Benjamin had sworn to Aisha that he'd call Boston General Hospital from school that day. He didn't want to risk phoning from home, where any number of people could "accidentally" overhear the conversation.

"Is this phone call long distance, by any chance?" Sandra asked.

Benjamin smiled. "Would I use precious school funds for my own selfish purposes?"

Sandra laughed. "Yes, but I'll let you call anyway. I was just on my way to lunch."

She guided Benjamin to the phone on her desk, then left him alone in the office. Benjamin sat in the secretary's chair, swiveling back and forth.

After a minute he picked up the receiver. His heart was beating wildly as he dialed the phone number he'd memorized. After two rings, a cool, professional-sounding person answered the phone.

Benjamin cleared his throat. "Hello. I'd like to speak to Dr. Rita Kaufman, please. I think I might be a candidate for her blindness reversal surgery."

Claire saw him when the *Minnow* was docking on the island. He was sitting on a bench, his head tilted toward the sun. She ran her fingers through her hair, then searched her pockets for lipstick.

She made herself walk slowly off the ferry. Now that the chase was over, she could afford to take her time.

Claire sat down on the far end of his bench. "You didn't have to wait for me."

He'd been staring in the opposite direction, toward the ferry. "Oh, hi, Claire." He smiled but kept his eyes fixed on the boat. "I didn't see you."

Claire frowned. He hadn't been waiting for her. He'd been waiting for Zoey.

"Well, here I am."

He smiled. "Hey, where's everyone else? Don't you guys usually take the ferry together?"

"In other words, where's Zoey?"

Aaron didn't miss a beat. "Sure, Zoey. And Nina. She didn't get off, either."

Claire decided to let the matter rest. She'd grill him about Zoey in a more private setting. "Zoey and Nina went to the mall. But they'll be over later."

He nodded.

Keep talking, Claire. He's not interested. "So, you want to see the coolest place on Chatham Island?"

"Why not?"

They said almost nothing as they walked the short distance to the Geigers' house, but Claire could tell that Aaron's interest was piqued as he followed her up to her room and then up the ladder that led to her widow's walk. Most people didn't have a trapdoor in their ceiling.

When they got outside, Claire inhaled the fresh, cold air. As always, she felt invigorated. "This is my favorite place in the world. I come up here at least twice a day."

"I can see why." Aaron walked to the edge of the widow's walk and rested his hands lightly on the railing.

"Oh, yeah? Why?" Claire stood just behind him. His hair curled over the top of his collar. It looked like silk.

"It's beautiful. You can see into forever."

"People think I'm strange for hanging out up here all the time." She moved next to him and looked beyond North Harbor to the ocean. The lighthouse rose up out of the water, a symbol of strength that somehow made her feel bolder.

This was her island. Her widow's walk. She would call the shots.

"Strangeness, like beauty, is in the eye of the beholder." Aaron moved his head slightly, and Claire found herself staring into his hazel eyes.

"What if I told you my dream is to move to Antarctica and study weather?" Claire moved her eyes back to the lighthouse. Looking at Aaron made her feel weak.

"I'd suggest you buy a warm parka and an extra pair of long johns."

"Is that all?" Claire asked.

"You want more?"

"You said you're into philosophy. Philosophize."

"Antarctica could get mighty lonely. Just you and some polar bears."

"Anyplace can be lonely."

"Now you sound like a philosopher."

"I'm a realist."

"Sounds like a pretty grim reality." He turned away from the view, looking instead at Claire. "Why Antarctica?"

She held her hands to the sky. "I want to study the weather. Bad weather." She shrugged. "What can I say? Storms are my deepest passion."

"Is there a storm coming, Claire?" Aaron asked.

Claire felt the pulse in her neck beating. "Sooner or later. A big one."

His smile was lazy, ironic. "Well, which is it? Sooner? Or later?"

Her throat was dry. "Judging from the air up here, I'm guessing sooner."

He moved his gaze for a moment. When he looked at her again, he was wearing the same

171

meaningless, pleasant expression he'd had at the dock.

"You've got it bad for Zoey, don't you?" Claire asked. When going for the jugular, she gave her opponent as little warning as possible.

"Zoey has a boyfriend." Aaron turned away from her. His back was rigid as he stared out at the velvet ocean.

"You're going to let that stop you?"

"Lucas is a good guy," he said blandly.

"You're avoiding the question." Claire felt slightly disappointed in Aaron.

"Zoey deserves the best." Aaron rested his elbows on the railing. His posture was casual and unconcerned. Suspiciously so.

"Is that supposed to be an answer?"

"If you want it to be."

Someone was pounding on Christopher's door. His first thought, when he saw Nina's pale face and red eyes, was that something was wrong with Aisha.

"What is it?" he asked, trying to force himself to continue breathing regularly.

When Nina didn't answer, he grabbed her arm. "Is Aisha hurt? Did she get in an accident?"

Nina pulled her arm away. "I wish."

Christopher backed up. Something was definitely wrong with Nina. She was pacing around the room muttering to herself. Her eyes had dark circles under them, and her hair resembled a badly constructed bird's nest. A nervous breakdown seemed to be in progress.

Now that he knew Aisha was okay, Christopher decided it would be best to sit on his bed and wait for her to speak.

When Nina turned to him, her face was like Mia Farrow's in *Rosemary's Baby*. "Christopher, how well do you know Aisha?"

"What?"

"Do you know what she does when she's not with you?" Nina's voice had a surreal quality that gave Christopher the chills.

"Pretty much, yeah." When they weren't together, Aisha was either at school, at home, or at Zoey's or Nina's.

"What if I told you that she's seeing someone on the side?"

Christopher felt the blood drain from his face. "Is this about that Jeff guy? Has she been talking to him?"

Nina snorted. "I'm talking about Benjamin."

Christopher laughed. "Benjamin? Get serious, Nina."

Benjamin was a cool guy. And even Christopher could recognize that a lot of women might find him attractive. But Benjamin wasn't a threat to Christopher.

"Laugh all you want, Christopher. It's true." She started pacing again.

"Nina, I think you're suffering from paranoia. Have you ever thought about taking Prozac?"

"I heard them talking in Benjamin's room. Shall I quote?" Nina asked.

"Please, be my guest."

"'You're turning me on,'" Nina said in a high, singsong voice. "'Shh. Someone might be listening.'" She paused. "Do you want me to go on?"

"No, thanks. I think I get the gist."

Nina waved her hands in the air. "Don't you *care*? Aren't you *upset*?"

"I'm sure there's a rational explanation." Christopher hoped he sounded more confident than he felt.

"I'm telling you, it's true."

"I trust Aisha. I'm not going to get all steamed up for no reason. She wouldn't appreciate it very much."

Nina went to the door. "Fine, be a fool. But I'm going to take action. I've got a plan." She left, slamming the door behind her.

When she was gone, Christopher sat on his bed. It wasn't true. Aisha would never betray him like that. Or Nina, for that matter.

Five minutes later he picked up the phone. Christopher felt slightly ridiculous for checking up on Aisha, but he couldn't help himself. He'd just say hi, then tell her all the stupid stuff Nina had been saying. After Aisha became totally indignant because he'd even entertained the idea that such a thing was possible, they'd have a good laugh. And then in the morning he'd stop by her house at the end of his paper route.

Aisha's little brother answered the phone on the third ring. "Hey, Kalif. What's shaking?" Christopher asked.

"*Nada mucho.* You see the game?"

"Nah. I was working."

"That's rough. The Chiefs killed the Cowboys. It was a massacre."

"So, is Aisha around?" Christopher asked.

"No, man, she's not here."

Christopher took a deep breath. There was nothing wrong with Aisha's not being at home. She wasn't *required* to be at home every minute that he wasn't with her. "Do you know where I can find her?"

"Uh, yeah. I think she said something about going to see Benjamin."

"Oh."

"Want me to tell her you called?"

"No, uh, I'm going to bed, anyway. I'll just talk to her tomorrow."

Christopher hung up the phone. He had to face the possibility that his girlfriend was in love with another guy. But Christopher wouldn't give up Aisha without a fight. When she realized how much he really loved her, there was no way she'd stay with Benjamin. Christopher wouldn't let that happen.

Jake's room was in the basement of the McRoyans' home, which was built on a hill. This was something he'd learned to appreciate over the last few years, especially when he'd wanted to sneak over to Zoey's late at night. Using the sliding glass door that led from his bedroom to the backyard, he could come and go without dealing with parental interrogation.

At midnight Jake stuffed a few pillows under his covers in case his mom decided to check on him. Then he turned out the light and stepped into the cold, dark night.

Jake felt nostalgic as he fell into a jog toward South Street. He'd run this same path hundreds of times, but this time he wasn't going to the Passmores' to see Zoey.

Lara had been on his mind since Sunday, when he'd recognized the same lost look in her eyes that he often saw when he gazed into a mirror. She obviously needed a friend, and so did Jake. Together they might be able to stave off loneliness—a state of being with which Jake had become intimately familiar.

At the Passmores' Jake hesitated for only a moment before taking the stairs to Lara's room two at a time. She'd hung a red cloth over her window, behind which Jake could see the glow from a lamp.

Jake wiped his sweaty palms against his jeans as he waited for her to open the door. He still wasn't sure what he planned to say to her, and he had no idea if she even wanted to see him.

When Lara answered the door, Jake's physical reaction was immediate. She wore nothing but a thigh-skimming T-shirt, and Jake was almost positive that she wasn't wearing a bra. He sucked in a deep breath, unprepared for the overwhelming physical attraction he felt for Lara.

"Jake," she said, leaning against the door jamb. "What are you doing here, Jake Jake Jake?"

"I, uh, wanted to see how you were doing."

She giggled. "Come in, Jake Jake Jake. I'm havin' a little party."

Jake frowned. Lara's voice was slightly slurred, and when she moved from the door to her bed, she swayed back and forth.

A half-empty twelve-pack of Heineken sat on the nightstand. Empty cans littered the room, and the air smelled as if the contents of one of the cans had landed on the floor.

"Lara, what are you doing in here?"

She popped open a beer and handed it to him. "The same thing we did on Halloween. Getting smashed." She laughed again, then downed the rest of the beer she was drinking.

Jake looked at the can of Heineken in his hand. It was lukewarm, but even so, he wanted to lift it to his mouth and let the beer pour down his throat. But he couldn't let himself fall into the trap. Once he started drinking, the monster inside would have to be fed over and over, until Jake himself was totally obliterated.

Jake forced himself to open the door and pour the beer over the side of the staircase. As the amber liquid splashed to the ground, disappearing into the dark grass, he felt a weight being lifted from his shoulders. He'd been tempted, but he'd stood his ground.

"I don't drink anymore, Lara," he said, tossing the empty into her miniature wastebasket. "I told you that."

She rolled her eyes. "Come on, jock boy. Let's party."

"You've had enough, Lara."

She stood up shakily and pulled him toward her. "We'll have a real good time," she whispered.

Her warm breath smelled like alcohol. Gently he pushed her away. "I want to get to know you, Lara. But not like this."

She sagged onto the bed. "I know you want me, and I know you want a beer."

Jake shrugged. He couldn't truthfully deny either of those claims.

Lara grabbed another Heineken. "So don't drink," she said. "I can still make you go home singing."

Jake felt his ears turning red. No girl had ever talked to him that way. "I think I'd better go now, Lara. I shouldn't have come in the first place."

When he put his hand on the doorknob, she jumped up and grabbed his arm. "Please don't go."

He shook his head. "If I stay . . . well, it's all too tempting."

Her face was sad as she let his arm drop

back to his side. "Fine. I don't need you or anybody else to enjoy myself."

Jake couldn't stop himself from taking a last look at the curve of her thighs and breasts. "Lara . . . if you decide you want to stop drinking, call me. I'll be there for you."

By the time Jake got home and took a cold shower, it was almost two o'clock in the morning. Still, he lay awake for a long, long time.

Fifteen

On Wednesday morning Christopher didn't stop at Aisha's at the end of his paper route. Five-thirty in the morning was not the time to knock on your girlfriend's window and ask her if it was true that she'd been messing around with another guy.

Besides, he was a man with a mission, and if it *was* true that Aisha was seeing Benjamin, he'd be too distracted to go on a job hunt. And getting another source of income would raise his self-esteem, which had been uncharacteristically lagging for the past few days. When dealing with a possible betrayal, it was always better to come from a position of strength.

He had the morning shift at Passmores', where he cooked with such intensity that Mr. Passmore asked him if he needed some herbal tea to mellow out a little. Christopher declined on the basis that he was not a mellow type. Nor did he want to be.

After his shift, Christopher drank two cups of coffee and scarfed down a three-egg Western omelet. Then he sprinted to his apartment, where he showered, shaved, and put on his one and only suit. He took a moment to glance in the mirror and admire how good he looked, then ran to the ferry as fast as he could without breaking into a sweat.

At two o'clock Christopher hopped off the bus at the Weymouth Mall. He planned to go into the first store he saw and ask for a job. If they said no, he'd go to the next. And the next. He hoped he wouldn't have to repeat the scenario too many times.

By four o'clock he had entered and exited forty-two stores. Only nine had even let him fill out an application, much less hired him. His suit was a bit crumpled, but Christopher managed to smile brightly as he walked into Cal's Computer World.

"Hi! Are you Cal?" he said to a fiftyish man who was sitting behind a counter.

"Yeah. Why?" The man looked him up and down suspiciously. "Are you selling something? 'Cause if you are—"

"Not some*thing*," Christopher said cheerfully. "Some*one*. Me."

"You're looking for a job?" Cal asked.

"That's right, sir." Christopher put on his widest, most charming grin—the one Aisha had finally given in to.

"What kind of computer training do you have?"

Christopher's smile froze. "Well, training in the formal sense of the word?"

"Right."

"Uh, none."

Cal nodded, as if he'd known the answer all along. "Sorry, buddy. You've got to be educated for a job like this."

Christopher cringed. "The whole reason I need a job is because I'm trying to save money for college. But how can I get an education if no one will give me a job?"

Cal shrugged. "What came first? The chicken or the egg?"

Christopher's shoulders slumped, and he abandoned his vain attempt at a smile. He felt utterly defeated. How could he convince Aisha that he was really and truly the only guy for her if he couldn't even get a lousy job as a salesman? He was a failure.

"Well, thanks anyway," he muttered bitterly.

As he moved to the door Cal called out to him, "Why don't you try next door? They're always looking for ambitious young men like yourself. And they'll pay for your education, too."

Christopher stared at him. "Are you serious, man?"

"Sure."

Christopher bolted out of the store. Finally things were looking up. He'd walk next door, march inside, and introduce himself. Cal might turn out to be a guardian angel disguised as an aging, balding white man.

Christopher stopped to check out the name of the place next door. When he saw where he was, his jaw dropped.

U.S. Army was written in huge letters on the window of a small store. From where he stood, Christopher could see a man in an olive green uniform shuffling papers on his desk.

Christopher laughed out loud. Cal, his guardian angel, had sent him to a United States Army recruiting office. This was the place where down-on-their-luck guys went to sign their life (not to mention their hair) away to a bunch of drill sergeants with sticks up their butts. This was the first step toward getting your head blown off in some far-off country where it was always hot outside. This was *not* a place for Christopher Shupe.

Christopher glanced at the guy inside, who looked as though he was perfectly happy being in the employment of the United States Army. Had *that* guy been down on his luck once?

Christopher reconsidered his line of thinking. The army was also the source of a very steady paycheck. And it was true that if a soldier stayed in long enough, he'd eventually get a college education, courtesy of the U.S. government. And there were health benefits and paid vacation, too.

What the hell? he thought. His day couldn't get any worse.

Christopher opened the door, and the young man at the desk snapped to attention.

"Good afternoon," he said, standing up. His hair was buzzed so close to his head that Christopher could see his scalp.

"Uh, hi." Christopher stood awkwardly. Was he supposed to salute or something?

On the walls of the office were a half-dozen posters of Uncle Sam pointing his index finger at the viewer. We Want You, the posters said in bold letters. Well, at least *somebody* did.

There were also photographs of smiling GIs in fancy, gold-buttoned uniforms. The men were standing against scenic backdrops in places such as Hawaii, Greenland, and Switzerland.

"What can I do for you?" The guy looked at him expectantly.

"I guess I'm interested in joining the army. Maybe."

The guy beamed. "Let me introduce myself." He extended his hand for Christopher to shake. "I'm Lieutenant Charles Lang."

Christopher shook his hand. "Nice to meet you. I'm Christopher Shupe."

The lieutenant sat back down behind his desk, indicating that Christopher should take the chair across from him. "Okay, Christopher. Let's talk about the army."

Half an hour later, Christopher's head was spinning. Lieutenant Lang had made the army sound like a day at Disneyland. He would develop his body into peak physical condition, learn about computers (take that, Cal), honor his country, and travel to exotic places. And he'd get paid a lot more than he could ever make cooking part time at the Passmores'.

The traveling-to-exotic-places part of the

deal bothered him. He liked adventure as much as the next guy, but traveling *anywhere* meant leaving Aisha behind. With Benjamin. The idea of that cozy setup made Christopher physically ill. As tempting as it sounded, there was no way he could join the army unless he could take Aisha with him. And that was impossible. Unless . . . The gears started turning in his mind. He was silent for a long time.

The lieutenant's voice broke into his thoughts. "Any questions, Christopher?"

"Just one." Christopher took a deep breath. "Do you have any special provisions for married recruits?"

Nina skipped school on Wednesday. She couldn't bear the idea of seeing Aisha and Benjamin again. The only way she'd gotten through the day before was by pleading cramps and spending most of the afternoon in the nurse's office. When the phone rang, again and again, during and after school, Nina let the machine pick up. After two calls from Benjamin and one from Zoey, she unplugged the answering machine.

On Wednesday evening Nina waited until dark to leave home. Dressed in black jeans, a black parka, and a black hat, she blended into the night, just as she'd planned.

At the Passmores', Nina crept up to the side of the house. Being careful not to crunch any leaves under the thick soles of her boots, she tiptoed to Benjamin's window.

He was inside, writing something on his computer. The only light in the room glowed from the eerie white screen. Nina leaned against the window to try to read whatever was on the monitor. She was so intent on her mission that she accidentally banged her head against the glass of the window.

Benjamin moved his head, turning away from the screen. He'd obviously heard her. "Damn," Nina whispered.

She stayed completely motionless, willing Benjamin to turn his attention back to the computer.

"Hello?" he called.

The only sound was Nina's breathing, and she hoped that Benjamin's hearing wasn't so finely tuned that he could pick it up from inside the house.

As Nina watched, Benjamin shook his head in confusion. Apparently he'd decided the noise was nothing. Nina felt like a louse for taking advantage of her boyfriend's blindness to spy on him—but what choice did she have?

After a few more minutes, she sneaked silently away from the window. Now she just had to wait for Aisha. As soon as that two-timing, back-stabbing ex–good friend arrived, Nina would make her move.

Nina hoped Aisha would show up sooner rather than later. It was freezing.

Sixteen

"So that's what Yeats is saying in 'Leda and the Swan'?" Aisha asked Zoey.

"Basically." Zoey was finally helping Aisha with her English assignment. She'd had to apologize daily since she'd blown her off on Saturday.

Zoey tossed Aisha *The Collected Poems of William Butler Yeats*. "Don't forget to return this."

Aisha stuffed the book into her already full backpack. "Hey, I *always* return books. Claire's the one who hoards them like acorns."

"Just a friendly reminder," Zoey said. "Sorry again about Saturday."

"You had a lot on your mind."

Zoey thought of Aaron's hazel eyes and his strong fingers digging in the sand. Then she thought about his lips. Specifically, she thought about his lips pressed against hers. What if Lucas found out? What if Aaron had told Aisha one night at the B&B, and she told Lucas? Zoey's life would enter disaster mode in two seconds.

"Did he say something to you?" Zoey studied Aisha's face for clues.

"He?" Aisha asked. "He who?"

Zoey cursed herself. Of course, Aisha was talking about the situation with Lara, not Aaron. "Nothing. I meant to say, you're right, I did have a lot on my mind."

"Whatever you say, Zo." Aisha raised an eyebrow, then opened the door. "See you tomorrow."

Benjamin was waiting behind the door of the family room. When he heard Aisha's footsteps, he poked his head into the front hall.

"Aisha?" he whispered.

He heard a gasp and then the sound of a bag crashing to the floor.

"Shh!" he hissed.

Aisha got closer. "Benjamin! You scared me."

"Sorry. I just didn't want Zoey to know that I was talking to you."

He heard her sharp intake of breath.

"Is it about . . . you know?"

"Yeah. Come to my room for a minute."

When they were in his room, Benjamin switched on his overhead light for Aisha's sake, then carefully closed his door. "I think I'm a go," he said.

Dr. Kaufman had asked him a million questions on the phone the previous day. With each answer she'd became more and more excited. That afternoon she'd faxed a bunch of forms to Sandra's office for him to fill out. He needed Aisha's help.

Aisha grabbed his shoulders. "Benjamin, this is incredible!" she shrieked.

Benjamin cringed. "I know, I know, but be quiet."

He heard Aisha sit down in the chair at his desk. "Tell me everything."

As soon as Aisha closed the door behind her, Zoey reached under her bed and pulled out the Bessie Smith CD she'd bought at the mall the day before. She ran her finger down the list of songs: "Down-Hearted Blues," "Jailhouse Blues," "Frosty Morning Blues." The songs had a definite theme. Zoey put the CD in her stereo and selected track number eleven, "Sinful Blues."

Bessie Smith's sad, gravelly voice filled her room. Zoey closed her eyes, listening to the woman Aaron had called the queen of the blues. The words were mournful. Bessie Smith ached for her lover, a man she couldn't have. Zoey could relate.

When the song ended, Zoey forced herself to turn off the stereo and open *The Scarlet Letter*. Her paper was due on Friday, and she hadn't even started. Zoey listlessly picked up the sheet that outlined the assignment:

PAPER TOPIC

Please write a 1,750-word essay about Nathaniel Hawthorne's classic, *The Scarlet Letter*. Pick one of the novel's major themes and develop a thesis based on your interpretation of Hawthorne's work. Make sure to build your argument with quotes from the text. Suggested themes include adultery, society, repression, and morality. No secondary sources required. Due in class on December 6. Late papers will be penalized.

Zoey crumpled up the sheet and stuffed it under her pillow. She'd worry about Hester and her big scarlet letter the next day. Adultery and morality simply weren't subjects Zoey felt like pondering.

Then she saw Aisha's mittens, which she'd left on top of Zoey's dresser. Zoey heaved herself off the bed. She'd put the mittens in her bag and give them to Aisha on the ferry.

Then again, the morning would probably be bitterly cold. And knowing Aisha, she wouldn't realize she'd forgotten the mittens at the Passmores' until she'd ransacked the whole inn looking for them. By that time, Aisha would be so late that she'd have to sprint all the way to the ferry.

If she were really and truly a good friend, she'd just take the mittens over to Aisha's that night. In fact, it would be a nice way to atone for her lapse on Saturday.

Zoey slipped on the mittens and headed downstairs. If she ran into Aaron at Aisha's, it would be sheer coincidence. Nothing more.

Jake lay on his bed watching *Road Rules*, MTV's new show that sent five young people across the United States in a souped-up

Winnebago. Jake liked Cat the best. She was from Atlanta and she had great breasts—at least from what he could tell on his nineteen-inch television screen.

He was supposed to be doing a paper on *The Scarlet Letter*, but when it came to English class, Jake rarely did what he was supposed to.

A knock on his sliding glass door made him jump. He hadn't had a late evening visitor since he and Claire broke up several weeks before. Actually, he hadn't had *any* visitors since he and Claire broke up.

Jake went to the door. Because his lights were on and the night was dark, for a moment he couldn't see who was outside. Then she came close to the door, and Lara's face appeared before him.

He opened the door, acutely aware that he was wearing only a pair of sweatpants. "Hey," he said.

She looked cold. Lara wasn't wearing a hat or gloves, and her thin leather jacket couldn't have been much protection from the frigid air. Her teeth were audibly chattering. "Hi, Jake."

He opened the door wider. "Come on in. You look like a human ice cube."

"I feel like one," she said, stepping into his room and glancing around. "Chatham's a lot colder than Weymouth."

Jake nodded, crossing his arms in front of his bare chest. "Yeah, well, there's a lot of wind. You get used to it."

She sat down in the chair next to his bed and rubbed her hands together. Her teeth were still chattering. Jake pulled the comforter from his bed and wrapped it around her shoulders.

"Thanks," she said. After that she was silent.

Jake sat down on his bed, facing the chair. Lara looked like a different girl that night. She had on no makeup, and her long dirty-blond hair was tied back in a ponytail. Most surprising, she was wearing a pair of baggy jeans and a faded blue sweatshirt.

"So, uh, are you okay? I mean, why'd you come all the way over here?"

When Lara looked up at him, her blue eyes reminded him exactly of Zoey's. "I wanted to apologize for last night," she said.

"Really? I mean, why?"

She buried her body deeper under the comforter. "I was totally out of control, Jake. I *am* totally out of control. I realized that when I woke up with one of the worst hangovers of my life this morning."

Jake knew what that felt like. His stomach heaved at the mere thought of the morning after the homecoming dance. He'd puked for hours. "That's rough. I've been there."

She nodded. "I know you have. . . . That's why I want your help."

"My help?" Jake leaned back on his bed. He couldn't remember the last time someone besides his mother had asked for his help. It felt good.

"Yeah. I, uh, want to stop drinking. I want to be a better person." She paused. "The kind of person Jeff Passmore would be proud to have as his daughter."

Jake was touched. Lara's vulnerability was written all over her face as she stared at him with those wide blue eyes. "I'll do anything I can, Lara. I swear."

A tear rolled down her cheek. "I know I can stop . . . if I just have someone to talk to when I'm lonely."

Jake felt a surge of affection that had nothing to do with his physical attraction to Lara. She was like a wounded bird on the side of the road. With a little tender loving care, she might learn to fly again—without the aid of alcohol.

Jake scooted forward and rested his hands on her shoulders. "We'll be there for each other, Lara. You'll never have to drink again."

The tears were flowing freely now. Jake even felt one or two well up in his own eyes. "Thank you," Lara whispered hoarsely.

Jake pulled her toward him, comforter and all. They fell in a heap on his bed, and Jake hugged her tight. That was all he intended to do—hug her, stroke her hair, promise her that he'd help her get her life back on track.

But her hair was so much softer than he'd expected that he couldn't stop touching it. He kissed her cheek, which was also silky smooth. He kissed her cheek again.

Then Lara kissed *his* cheek. Several times.

Jake rubbed his hands up and down her back, shoving away the comforter as he did so. A moment later, a shock went through him as he felt Lara's hands, now warm, on the skin of his chest.

His lips traveled slowly from her cheek to her lips to her neck, and then back to her lips. He could still feel her tears as she kissed him back hungrily.

Nina's Plan

1. Read up on Eric and Lyle Menendez. Find out how to make a jury believe I was justified in killing.

2. Read up on O. J. Simpson. Try to obtain celebrity status. Find out how much Johnnie Cochran charges per hour.

3. Dig up old Clue game. Decide whether to use the candlestick, the lead pipe, the revolver, or whatever else Colonel Mustard was axed with.

4. Complain of PMS so much that after the murder, people can testify about it in court.

5. Confront Aisha and Benjamin. Tell them what scum they are.

6. Kill them both, according to research results from step three.

7. Claim insanity. Get off with the help of a good lawyer and Dad's money.

8. Write a best-selling book about my life. Move to New York and live off the millions of dollars in royalties.

9. Die bitter and heartbroken, stray cats my only company.

Seventeen

Did frostbite start in the fingers or the toes? Nina tried to wiggle her toes, which had been numb for at least thirty minutes. And the backs of her calves weren't doing too well. She'd been crouching behind a bush across the street from the Passmores' house for what felt like her entire lifetime.

Aisha had shown up quite a while ago, but the girl was even sneakier than Nina had guessed. Instead of going straight to Benjamin's room, she had gone into Zoey's bedroom, where Nina had seen her through the window. She and Benjamin would probably wait for Zoey to go to bed, then meet for a midnight make-out session. And Nina didn't care if she *did* have to wait until midnight to confront them. Nothing was going to stop her.

Sitting there, she'd gone over the events of her sixteen years on the planet, detail by detail. She'd just begun reviewing the grisly story of how Aisha and Benjamin had stabbed her in the back when the Passmores' front door opened— the first sign of life from the house since Lara had left fifteen minutes earlier. Zoey walked out carrying something small and dark in her hands. She glanced up and down the block, then jogged quickly down the street. Nina didn't have time to wonder where Zoey was going at nine o'clock on a Wednesday night.

This was it. The moment of truth. Zoey had left, but Aisha was still inside. Undoubtedly she was with Benjamin. They'd probably started making out the minute Zoey had put her coat on. By now they could be to second base.

Nina didn't bother to spy on her low-life ex-friend and soon-to-be ex-boyfriend through Benjamin's window. She already knew what she'd see.

She turned the knob on the Passmores' front door slowly. She wanted to be as quiet as possible. In a situation like this, the element of surprise was a key factor.

Nina crouched outside Benjamin's room, her ear pressed to the door.

"Aisha, you're sure Zoey doesn't know you're in here, right? She'd know we were up to something if she found you."

Nina heard Aisha made an exasperated noise. "I'm positive. She probably thinks I'm home by now."

"Good," Benjamin said.

"But we need to tell her soon, Benjamin. We need to tell *everyone*. Now that you've decided you're really going through with this thing, Nina deserves to know the truth."

200

Outside the door, Nina sank to the floor. She didn't try to stop the tears.

Benjamin held up his hand. "Aisha, do you hear something?"

Aisha stopped talking. At first the house seemed completely silent. But after a few moments, Aisha heard a sort of moaning sound—something between a cat howling and a baby crying, only much quieter. The noise seemed to be coming from just outside Benjamin's door.

"Yeah, I hear it." She listened again. "Do you think it's Lara?"

Benjamin shook his head. "I have no idea. But we'd better find out who—or *what*—it is."

Aisha got up and opened the door. For about half a second she didn't see anyone. The hall looked empty. Then she looked down. Nina was at her feet, huddled in the fetal position.

"Nina!" she yelled. "What's wrong?"

Nina opened her eyes, which were red and swollen. "Don't talk to me, Aisha," she croaked.

Benjamin came to the door. He seemed unable to identify Nina's exact whereabouts. "She's on the floor," Aisha explained.

Benjamin knelt down. "Nina, tell us what's wrong. What is it?"

"*You're* what's wrong!" Nina screamed. "You and my so-called friend Aisha."

"Nina, are you insane?" Aisha shouted.

"Insane, ha!" Nina stood up, wiping the tears from her face.

Benjamin tried to put an arm around her, but she jerked away. "Nina, I don't understand—"

"Don't bother with the lies," Nina shouted. "I heard you two."

"Heard us?" Aisha asked. She was getting more bewildered by the second.

"Yesterday. You two were talking about kissing and touching. I was standing right outside the door."

Aisha thought back to the previous day. She'd come over to see if she could convince Benjamin to call Boston General. After a while he'd finally sworn on his music collection that he would call from school on Wednesday. Then they'd cruised the Internet, checking out a bunch of different chat sessions. . . . Suddenly Aisha realized what was going on.

"You can cut out the innocent act, Aisha," Nina was saying. "I'm not buying it."

Nina looked from Benjamin to Aisha. For two people who had just gotten caught betraying her, their remarkable calm was insulting.

Then, to Nina's horror, Benjamin laughed.

"Aisha's been helping me navigate the Internet," he said. "I've needed access to it for a project I'm working on."

"Is that what they're calling it these days?" She knew she sounded like a character from a bad 1940s movie, but she couldn't stop herself. She didn't *want* to stop herself.

"Nina, he's telling you the truth." Aisha

moved to Benjamin's desk and picked up a stack of paper.

Benjamin did not look at all ruffled, although he did appear the slightest bit irritated. Nina let herself wallow in the tiny hope that Benjamin and Aisha were telling the truth.

"So why were you talking about turning each other on and making plans to meet somewhere more private?"

Benjamin tried one more time to put an arm around Nina. This time she let it stay. "When we were through with my, uh, project, I had Aisha check out one of the chat rooms."

"So what?"

"So did you hear *me* saying any of those things?"

"No, just Aisha. But you were laughing and—"

"She was *reading* to me, Nina. Just like you always do."

Nina wanted to believe him. She wanted to believe both of them.

"So what's this project? Why couldn't I have helped you with it?"

He turned and put a hand on each of her shoulders. "You would have been too emotionally involved."

"I don't understand." Nina's brain felt as though it were going to explode.

Benjamin took a deep breath, then exhaled slowly. "Nina, there's a chance I'm going to be able to see again."

"What?"

"Some experimental surgery is being done in Boston. The doctors involved think they might be able to reverse my blindness."

Nina looked to Aisha, who nodded. "It's true. Benjamin didn't want to get anyone's hopes up before he knew whether or not he could really be a candidate for the surgery. Not even Zoey knows about this."

In the last five minutes, Nina had gone from thinking her boyfriend had dumped her to finding out that not only had he not cheated, but one day he might be able to see again. And the reason that he hadn't told her was because he'd wanted to spare her feelings.

Nina threw her arms around Benjamin's neck and covered his face with kisses. He hugged her, rocking gently back and forth. As Nina stood there, she knew she should be elated. Regaining his sight was something Benjamin had never even dared to dream about. She should be breaking out the champagne, or at least whooping and hollering.

But despite her smile on the outside, Nina wasn't elated. She was scared.

Nina glanced at Aisha, who had a few tears trickling down her face. "I'll leave you guys alone now," Aisha said, walking to the door.

Watching her, Nina remembered her conversation with Christopher the previous night. Big mistake. "Ah, Eesh?"

Aisha turned. "Yeah?"

"I'm really sorry that I suspected you of

trying to steal my boyfriend. You're the best, most understanding friend in the world for not being mad at me."

Aisha shrugged. "No harm done. Besides, I know what it's like when you suspect your boyfriend is with someone else." She shuddered. "It's a living hell."

Nina grimaced. "Speaking of your boyfriend, you might want to give Christopher a call."

Eighteen

Claire stared at the screen of her computer. She'd been sitting at her desk for over an hour, and so far she'd only typed the first sentence of her paper.

"'In *The Scarlet Letter,* Nathaniel Hawthorne depicts a society in which rigid moral standards override the importance of simple human compassion,'" she read aloud.

Not exactly Pulitzer prize-winning material. But Claire couldn't muster much intellectual interest in Hester Prynne and her doomed love affair. Another, currently nonexistent love affair was a more pressing concern.

Claire didn't bother to save the uninspired opening of her English paper before she switched off the computer. She'd start over the next day.

Claire glanced around her room, trying to find something that would hold her attention. Her eyes stopped at her overflowing bookcase. On the top shelf, shoved in between *Wuthering Heights* and *A Tale of Two Cities,* was Aisha's dog-eared copy of *Jane Eyre.*

Claire had borrowed the book over a year

before. Now she moved to the bookshelf and pulled it out. *Aisha probably wants this back,* she told herself.

Claire flopped on her bed and leafed through the story of Jane's trials and tribulations with Mr. Rochester. Aisha had highlighted several of the more dramatic passages, and there were cryptic notes scrawled in the margins.

She'd had the book for too long, Claire realized. There was nothing more annoying than a book borrower who had a tendency to assimilate the loaner's book into her own collection.

Claire stood up, clutching *Jane Eyre* as if the book might get up and walk away. She'd be a good friend (and borrower) by going straight to Aisha's house and returning the novel.

And if she happened to run into Aaron while she was there . . . well, that would be sheer coincidence. Nothing more.

Zoey rang the doorbell at the Grays'. She held the mittens in front of her, proof that she had a valid excuse to go all the way over there on a Wednesday night.

Kalif answered the door. "Hey, Zoey."

"Hey. I just, uh, wanted to bring Aisha her mittens. She left them at my house."

Kalif looked confused. "She's still at your house."

It was Zoey's turn to look confused. "She is?"

"I thought so."

Zoey realized that Aisha had probably stopped by Christopher's on the way home but wanted her mother to think she was still at the Passmores'. "Oh, right. You know, she actually had to go to Claire's. Something about a homework assignment."

Kalif shrugged. "Whatever."

Zoey was conscious of the mittens, which she still clung to. "Well, I'll just go put these in Aisha's room. I don't mind doing it myself. Not at all."

"Suit yourself," Kalif answered. He moved away from the door so that Zoey could come in, then disappeared in the direction of the kitchen. Zoey was alone.

She went first to Aisha's room. She put the mittens in the middle of the bed, where Aisha would be sure to see them. Then she sat in Aisha's desk chair, battling with herself over whether or not she should go say hi to Aaron.

After two minutes Zoey admitted to herself that this was a battle that had been lost before it even began.

She tiptoed through the house. Having Aisha's parents—or worse, Sarah Mendel—pop out and see her would put a crimp in her plan. She could just imagine the conversation that would take place between herself and Aaron's mother. *Hi, Ms. Mendel. We met at Thanksgiving. Now I'm sneaking into your son's room despite the fact that I have an awesome boyfriend. Good night.*

Zoey held her breath as she tapped lightly on Aaron's door. He answered immediately.

"Uh, hi," she said. "I was just, you know, bringing Aisha's mittens over because she left them at my house. Anyway, I don't want to bother you. I just, like, thought I would say hi and stuff. So, uh, hi."

Someone, please make me stop babbling, she prayed.

Aaron smiled. "Hi yourself." He took her hand and pulled her gently inside the room.

After he shut the door, Aaron held out his arms. Zoey melted into them. He didn't try to kiss her. He just hugged her close, whispering her name over and over.

Finally Zoey pulled away. "I shouldn't have come here."

"No?" Aaron asked quietly.

She went to the far side of the room and sat down in one of the inn's many overstuffed armchairs. The only other option was the bed, and Zoey thought that was the last place she should be.

"No. I mean, I wanted to see you, but I shouldn't." She looked at his guitar, which was leaning up against the wall. The memory of him singing to her made her heart hurt.

"You shouldn't?" Again his voice was quiet and calm.

"Aaron, I have a boyfriend."

"I know. Lucas." He stayed exactly where he was, regarding her with a steady gaze.

"He's really in love with me. We're a couple."

Aaron nodded. "And you're in love with him." It was a statement, not a question.

Zoey covered her face with her hands. She blinked back hot tears. "Yes. I mean, no. I don't know."

"Zoey, I'm not the kind of guy who goes around stealing other guys' girlfriends."

Zoey nodded miserably. "I know. And I'm not the kind of girl who goes around kissing guys who aren't her boyfriend."

Aaron picked up his guitar and ran his fingers lightly over the strings. "I wish I didn't feel about you the way that I do."

"How . . . how do you feel?" He voice and her hands were shaking. She stuck her hands between her knees.

Aaron played a riff from the eight-bar blues song he'd sung the other night. "I'm in love with you."

Zoey thought she might faint. She put her head down on her knees and sucked in huge breaths of air. She shouldn't have come. She should have stayed at home and written an incisive, scintillating paper about the repercussions Hester Prynne faced as a result of her adulterous affair. Or she should have called Lucas and asked him to come over. Anything but this heart-wrenching, mind-altering catastrophe.

She wanted to kiss him. She wanted to dig her fingers into his thick sweater and into his beautiful hair. She wanted to feel his lips. Not

211

just a chaste peck, but a real, soul-searching, spine-tingling kiss. His full mouth seemed to be a magnet.

Aaron set down the guitar and moved to the window. "Are you going to say anything?" he asked.

Zoey shook her head. "I don't know." His face was so serious that she felt fresh tears well up in her eyes.

"I'm not going to ask you to leave Lucas for me, Zoey. It wouldn't be fair."

Zoey stared at him. The need to kiss him was too overpowering. She felt as though she were in a desert and Aaron were water. Zoey found herself standing up, then walking toward him.

He turned from the window and looked into her eyes. She leaned against him, inhaling the clean, masculine smell of his sweater.

When he kissed her, Zoey didn't even try to resist.

Aisha's house was at the top of a steep hill, aptly named Climbing Way. Claire didn't make the trek to the Grays' house often. She preferred to let her friends come to her.

But lately Claire had been doing lots of things that she normally wouldn't even contemplate. Falling in love, for instance.

The night was cold and clear. Claire stopped for a moment, feeling the air around her. The temperature was probably about thirty-three degrees Fahrenheit. Close to freezing, but not quite there.

The house came into view when she was halfway up Climbing Way. There were lights on in almost every room, but from where she was, Claire couldn't see any movement inside the house.

Claire went over her plan as she climbed the last bit of the hill.

She hoped that Aisha wouldn't answer the door. Assuming she didn't, Claire would ask if Aisha was home, then "get lost" on the way to her room. If Aisha did answer, Claire would have to hang out with her for a while. Then she'd "get lost" on her way out. Either way, Claire would eventually find herself in Aaron's room.

Claire stopped just outside the inn. She scanned the second-floor windows, trying to figure out which might be Aaron's. Getting lost in the house would be a lot easier if she actually knew where she was going.

Her heart palpitated when she saw him. He was standing at his window, his back to her. Because his light was on and it was so dark outside, Claire could see him perfectly. She recognized his white cable-knit sweater, the one he'd worn to her party on Friday night.

Another figure came to the window. A girl. Zoey.

Claire watched as Aaron put his arms around Zoey's waist. Zoey took a step closer, burying her face in the thick knit of Aaron's sweater. With one hand he tilted her chin so that she was looking into his eyes. Up until this point, Claire was still breathing.

Aaron bent his head, then kissed Zoey on the lips. Claire's lungs seemed to collapse inside her chest. As the kiss continued, Claire saw Zoey's hands moving up and down Aaron's back. Her fingers stroked the soft, dark curls of his hair.

Moments later they moved away from the window. *To the bed,* Claire guessed. Through the window, Claire could see only a patch of bare wall. The square of light was as empty as Claire felt inside.

Claire waited there for a long time. But Zoey didn't come out.

Look out for . . .

MAKING OUT 10

At first **Nina** thought **Ben** was fooling around with **Aisha**. But then she discovered the truth: **Ben's** facing a decision that could change his life for ever. And she's scared he'll leave her unless . . .

Nina shapes up

Available March 1996

Look out for . . .

MAKING OUT 11

Aisha found out first and she told Nina, who had to tell Zoey, who let it slip to Lucas. Now Ben's big secret isn't a secret any more and they're all waiting to see what will happen when . . .

Ben takes a chance

Available April 1996

Look out for . . .